1,00

Get Your
Coventry Romances
Home Subscription NOW

And Get These
4 Best-Selling Novels
FREE:

LACEY
by Claudette Williams

THE ROMANTIC WIDOW
by Mollie Chappell

HELENE
by Leonora Blythe

THE HEARTBREAK TRIANGLE
by Nora Hampton

A Home Subscription! It's the easiest and most convenient way to get every one of the exciting Coventry Romance Novels! ...And you get 4 of them FREE!

You pay nothing extra for this convenience; there are no additional charges...you don't even pay for postage! Fill out and send us the handy coupon now, and we'll send you 4 exciting Coventry Romance novels absolutely FREE!

SEND NO MONEY, GET THESE

FOUR BOOKS FREE!

- - - - - - - - - - - - - - - - - - - -

C0181

MAIL THIS COUPON TODAY TO:
**COVENTRY HOME
SUBSCRIPTION SERVICE
6 COMMERCIAL STREET
HICKSVILLE, NEW YORK 11801**

YES, please start a Coventry Romance Home Subscription in my name, and send me FREE and without obligation to buy, my 4 Coventry Romances. If you do not hear from me after I have examined my 4 FREE books, please send me the 6 new Coventry Romances each month as soon as they come off the presses. I understand that I will be billed only $10.50 for all 6 books. There are no shipping and handling nor any other hidden charges. There is no minimum number of monthly purchases that I have to make. In fact, I can cancel my subscription at any time. The first 4 FREE books are mine to keep as a gift, even if I do not buy any additional books.

For added convenience, your monthly subscription may be charged automatically to your credit card.

☐ Master Charge   ☐ Visa

Credit Card # _____

Expiration Date _____

Name _____

Please Print)

Address _____

City _____ State _____ Zip _____

Signature _____

☐ Bill Me Direct Each Month

This offer expires March 31, 1981. Prices subject to change without notice. Publisher reserves the right to substitute alternate FREE books. Sales tax collected where required by law. Offer valid for new members only.

OLIVIA

Jennie Gallant

FAWCETT COVENTRY • NEW YORK

OLIVIA

Published by Fawcett Coventry Books, a unit of CBS Publications, the Consumer Publishing Division of CBS Inc.

ISBN: 0-449-50155-8

Printed in the United States of America

First Fawcett Coventry printing: January 1981

10 9 8 7 6 5 4 3 2 1

Chapter One

I CALL MY STEPMOTHER Doris. I cannot well call her Mrs. Fenwick, and refuse to use the term Mama. Doris has not changed over the year I have been away, confirming me in the opinion that I was wise to leave home. When a father on the windy side of sixty takes up with a vulgar widow at least twenty years his junior, it bodes ill for the peace of the family. Doris disliked me from the start, and the feeling was entirely mutual. Her dislike could not take, to a lady in her twenty-third year, the form of outright abuse. My character is strong enough that I am not likely ever to become an abused anything. No, she was stiffly polite, always deferring to me as though I were a guest in my own house. The resulting discomfort was enough to convince me I must leave, and leave I did, twelve months and one week ago.

There were no fireworks attendant on my departure. There was no reason why the daughter of the Dean of Bath should leave under a cloud. I made a grand and public affair of my departure. While the Dowager Marchioness of Monterne was holidaying at Bath to relieve her gout, she naturally called on me. I used the word "naturally" to introduce a little hidden cachet into my background. My late Mama, you see, was kin to the Monternes. My name is Olivia Fenwick, but my blood is half Monterne blue blood. I own life might have been more pleasant had my parents' blood been reversed—Papa the one with the noble pedigree—but it was not the case, and the Fenwicks, as you perhaps know, are not a contemptible line either. To return to our sheep—the Dowager wanted a companion for her daughter, who remained, at eighteen, almost completely innocent of education and polish. She was one of those Tally ho! girls, who reeked always of the stable, in both her personal perfume and her conversation.

Nominally a "companion," I was in fact a model and mentor for the girl. Doris had a going away party for me before I left in my cousin's crested carriage for the trip to Dawlish, her home in Devon. The present Marquess, her son, was only thirteen years old, and away at school, which made it eligible for her to continue as mistress of Dawlish, which is a beautiful old stone castle on the east bank of the Exe River.

I introduced Lady Deborah to the niceties of entering a room at a pace less than a gallop, of curtseying in lieu of wrenching a gentleman's hand from his wrist when he made her acquaintance, of reading something other than the Gentlemen's magazines, of dancing, of conversing in sentences instead of her more customary bellow of "Righto" or "I say." The visit had a greater success than either I or the Marchioness foresaw. At the end of nine months, Lady Deborah had attracted the attentions of no less a personage than an earl, fast on his way to becoming a duke, for his father, the Duke of Tavistock, was in his seventies. The head reels to think of Deborah being a duchess, but then what I have seen of duchesses at Dawlish has disillusioned me somewhat from considering them better than the rest of womankind. The Duke of Tavistock's lady, for example, regularly served watered wine, and had great gaping holes in the heels of her stockings, but that is neither here nor there. And besides, she had only married into the nobility. She was plain Miss Armitage before the wedding.

When the nuptials of Lady Deborah to Lord Strathacona took place last month, I was one of the bridesmaids at the elaborate do. My cousin, Lady Monterne, requested me to remain with her afterwards for the purpose of adding a touch of polish to her next daughter, but as Sylvia is only fifteen, there is little to be done in that corner yet. "I hate to lose you, my dear," she told me, "for it is certainly due to your work that our Deb fared so well. Must you go home to Bath then? So very unpleasant for you."

Lady Monterne had met Doris while in Bath, and knew whereof she spoke. She stated categorically that Papa ought to have been committed to Newgate for bringing the woman into the family. I am not sure in my own mind whether Bedlam would not be a more appropriate reward. "No, I cannot return to Bath," I told her. "You would not happen to know of anyone requiring a superior lady governess for her children?"

The question was a joke. A young lady like myself with some dowry (from Mama's portion) and a somewhat illustrious pedigree does not hire herself out. The word "governess" was sometimes used between us in a facetious way, however, to indicate the favor I did them. What I actually had in mind was another pleasant home as a companion to some of the nubility, as the Duchess of Tavistock calls the unwed daughters of herself and her noble friends.

It had not escaped my notice that very interesting

gentlemen were encountered in this sort of society, much more interesting than those that inhabited Bath. There could hardly be a *less* interesting assortment of gentlemen anywhere than hang out at Bath. They are of two main types: they either look and speak like women, or Irish chairmen.

Lady Monterne, not a terribly bright woman, took me at my word and reamed off a list of acquaintances looking out for a governess, causing me to correct her as to my meaning. "Oh," she said, surprised. "I am sure you are a dozen times better than the best governess *I* ever hired, my dear, and I should not have minded in the least paying you."

"*I* should mind the degradation of being a paid employee, however," I pointed out. "My own governess was hardly considered a part of the family. She was a servant, and treated as such."

"Certainly you would not want that, but it has never been the way *we* treat our governesses. They were always a part of the family, eating with us, traveling with us, going to the concerts and a few parties as well if they wished. But of course we were always very select in our choice of governesses for the girls. Only from the best families, but from an impoverished branch. One could not treat a Wilmot or a Fotheringham lady as hired help after all," she added, to clinch the matter. "Miss Wilmot had her own mount, in fact, and when she married later on, Debbie was a flower girl."

This was a form of condescension never encountered in any governess *I* had ever heard of, but there was no reason to doubt her word. The aristocracy may be as eccentric as they please; it is only the genteel middle class who cater to convention. "I should certainly demand a wage in the next house I went to if I were you. And *I* shall pay you too, Olivia," she declared. That she never did it is beside the point. It was her intention.

I remembered her words as I returned to Bath. Actually I had performed a considerable service for the Monternes in training Deborah, and my reward was a free trip home in the family carriage. Why should I give my services away? No one ever gave me anything. Indeed, what is given freely is less appreciated than what we pay for. Yes, certainly I would ask a wage next time I went as a companion.

It chanced the second day I was home I was shopping on Milsom Street to refurbish the lace and ribbons on a few gowns. We did not often get shopping from Dawlish, as the closest town was some miles distant. I stepped into Fabers Drapery Shop to peruse the wares, and overheard a conversation between two matrons. It was muslin they were discussing. Muslin, like people, comes in all styles and qualities.

"I like the rose sprigged," one woman said, "but it is only five shillings the yard. It cannot be a good quality."

"This at nine *looks* like it, but it must be better. It is Indian muslin," her friend said.

The shopkeeper came up to them to point out a more expensive batch of ells. He had muslin ranging up to fifteen shillings a yard, which, he assured them, was purchased by only his most discerning customers.

The women happily laid out their fifteen shillings for muslin which, upon my examination, looked very little different from the nine shilling, though I must own it was finer than the five shilling bolts, and more tightly woven. I let the man think I too was interested in purchasing muslin, but I was busy making an analogy to those skills I had decided to put out to hire. "Do you really think it is worth the difference in price?" I asked him, listening with some amusement for his answer.

"Certainly it is," he assured me. "Everyone knows the price of my muslins. If you want to be seen in the cheap stuff, it is your own affair, but you will be better thought of if you buy the fifteen shilling quality. The pattern is different, you see. It is easily distinguishable from the cheap."

The pattern was the only distinction I could see. For having the flowers a different shape (no prettier either), gullible women were paying out more than half again what the cloth was worth. "I rather like this one," I said, making a game of it, and pointing to the nine shilling bolt.

He gave me such a knowing look! You can afford no better, the look said. It was little short of contempt. "Will it be the *cheap* one then?" he asked, condescension written all over his face.

"Do you really think the other is worth the price?" I persisted, curious to hear what reason he would proffer, for I knew his answer would be in the affirmative.

"We all want to be well thought of. Folks judge by what they see on your back. The ladies seem to think it's worth it," he told me.

I said I would consider the matter further, and left, pondering his words. It gave a new light to my going out for hire. The more I puffed myself off, the likelier it was I would be appreciated. Yes, I would not humbly apply for any position through the good offices of Lady Monterne or her friends. I would let it be known to society at large in a discreet advertisement that a lady of superior attainments was considering to take charge of one or two young ladies providing the young ladies came up to her expectations. Only the most élite need reply, in other words.

I trust I do not overstate my credentials to say I am a lady of superior attainments. As the daughter of Dean Fenwick and a cousin of Lady Monterne, I fancy I am a cut above the average governess. I have spoken French from four years of age, for my mother was an advocate of early education for children. Indeed for quite seven years we housed a French orphan of good family to act as my playmate, for the very purpose of making me fluent in French. I have read widely in the classics and poetry, can (with considerable effort and a liberal use of the dictionary) manage to get an Italian piece into tolerable English. I have studied painting and music, and dote on Shakespeare. It was said that my rendition of Juliet at Miss Leigh's Seminary in Bath was better than the professional performance of the same role given in the Bath theater that year. As her fellow actor was the ridiculous Romeo Coates, however, it must be allowed she was working under a considerable handicap.

My mother introduced me to the progressive educational ideas of Mary Wollstonecraft, contained in her *Vindication of the Rights of Women.* Mama made the acquaintance of the female novelist, Jane Austen, when she was residing at Bath, and introduced me to her. She was kind enough to praise a poem I had written, but I was little more than a child at the time, and make no claim to being a poet. Neither ought half the people who have managed to get their scribblings into print, in my humble opinion. Wordsworth is sensitive and intelligible, to judge from his verse; Coleridge inventive, and for the rest of them—pshaw! If "The Corsair" had been written by Mr. Byron instead of Lord Byron, it would moulder unpublished, where it belongs. Lord Byron has created a deal of mischief with his demonic heroes.

Well, I trust the above gives a fair idea of what I mean to offer to the public, at my own price and on my own terms. My muslin will be sprigged with blossoms unseen on the five shilling bolt. If anyone is inclined to pay four hundred guineas a year for my services, she may have me. I mean to offer as well a rigorous physical regime to my charge (or charges, but two is the maximum number of girls). It is unhealthy in the extreme for young ladies to be bent over a tambour frame for hours a day. I do not excel as a horsewoman. Bath is a difficult city in which to negotiate on horseback, all hills and ups and downs. One is fagged to death before she hits the clean countryside. I am an expert walker, and mean to put the legs of my charges to work, filling their lungs with fresh air, and their cheeks with roses. I also have a book given me by the Duchess of Tavistock outlining calisthenics designed to develop the arms, torso and legs. Her girls are certainly well developed. A very good lithe figure Dulcinea has, and it is a pity she has a face like a horse to go with it. I envisage my course as being similar to a French finishing school, where a young lady might profitably spend a year between the schoolroom and the drawing rooms of society. I recall from my own presentation five years ago the gaucherie of many of the girls making their come out. It was thought I would make a good match at the time, but Papa fell ill before I was there three weeks, and so my visit was cut short.

Doris remonstrated with me in a purely mechanical way for my decision to leave home again. "I hope it is not on my account you go, Miss Fenwick," she said. Miss Fenwick, and she my stepmother for over a year.

"Certainly not, Doris," I assured her.

"You are more than welcome to stay on here."

"I want to go. Life is dull, tiresome for me in Bath with nothing to do. I shall be much happier in London, with plays and parties, you know."

"But to go as a governess—I am afraid your papa is not pleased. Will a governess be invited to parties?" she asked.

"This governess will be. I mean to make certain stipulations in the contract before I accept it. I must have a full day a week off to pursue my own interests. I

12

shall eat with the family, attend their larger social functions, have unlimited access to the library, wear what I wish, and be allowed to keep my own tilbury, which I mean to put at the disposal of my charges. I shall take them out with me in it, thus freeing the family carriage for the lady of the house. I cannot think many governesses offer so much."

"My, setting up your own tilbury!" Doris exclaimed. "When did you take this decision?"

The decision had evolved from Miss Wilmot's having her own mount. I do not ride well, but I am a fair fiddler, as no less a driver than Deborah's groom was kind enough to tell me. My last year's allowance had hardly been touched at Dawlish. The Monternes did not pay me, but they paid everything else, all those incidental expenses incurred in the normal course of life. It had occured to me that a lady would have little access to the delights of the city if she had no carriage. Then too, to come with my own tilbury would definitely set me apart from an ordinary governess. Really using the term governess for the total charge of the family's young females I intended taking was not accurate, but the word would be used in spite by some, and by acknowledging it myself, I could defang the vipers.

"I just decided yesterday," I told Doris.

"Have you had any offers of a job?" she asked.

"The advertisement appears in the London papers for the first time tomorrow. I shall go to London and conduct interviews at the Pulteney Hotel." Taking a room at the fabulous Pulteney was a wicked extravagance, but set the tone I wished for my new enterprise.

"The Pulteney—oh my!" Doris exclaimed, her fingers flying to her mouth in a common way, that set my nerves on edge. How different she was from Mama, who would laugh and make light of this spree I was embarking upon. But Doris was firmly rooted in the

13

genteel middle class. "It seems so *odd,* buying a carriage and going to the Pulteney, only to get a job."

"A position, Doris. Not a job. There is a difference."

"Very likely," she admitted, smiling apologetically, and batting her eyes. She has pretty eyes, that are unfortunately devoid of expression. "So you are definitely leaving us again then?"

"Yes, but I shall write, and it would be nice if you would write me once in a while too, Doris, to let me know how Papa goes on, for he is a terrible noodle, you know, and waits an age before answering my letters."

"Yes," she said diffidently. She had written me exactly one note during my year at Dawlish. The less said about its execution the better. She soon left the room, relief evident on every line of her face.

There was no going away party on this occasion. I was not home long enough to look up my old friends, with the exception of Mrs. Crewe, my late mother's best friend. She was to accompany me to the Pulteney, for I could not like to appear unchaperoned, a single lady not quite old enough to jaunter about the countryside alone. She had relatives in the city who were to help me with the purchase of my tilbury, and return with her to Bath later for a visit. Of the greatest importance, she was extremely elegant. When my mama passed away, she inherited the title of the best-dressed lady in Bath (where the competition, of course, is not strenuous). We were to take up residence at the Pulteney for a week, where I would sit like a spider in a web, awaiting my prey.

Chapter Two

I WAS TREATED AS some sort of resident freak at the Pulteney. One shy chambermaid told me no lady had received more mail since the Grand Duchess Catherine of Oldenberg had refused accommodation at the Palace and taken lodgings there during the state visit. That was the sort of clientele they had at the place, stuffed full of princes and foreign royalty. It is really astonishing how many ladies were eager to pay a sum which I must allow to be mildly excessive for my services. I later learned the Marchioness had been busy on my behalf. She dropped a letter to her crone, Lady Glanmore, a society leader who was blessed with no less than four graceless daughters, that I was a sort of clever companion cum matchmaker, and it was certainly a matchmaker that beleaguered parent required. A miracle maker would have been even better. One glimpse of her girls was enough to determine me against entering her household. To call them plain was to be kind, and not quite truthful, for they went a good deal beyond plain. All the way to ugly, in fact. A pair of twins pushing seventeen, one a year older, and one I am quite certain was at least my own age. She was introduced as "the eldest, already come out a year ago, or was it two, Lady Lucy?" Lady Lucy blushed and snickered, and kept the dark secret.

I explained that it was younger girls I was interested in. She offered me, without a word of exaggeration, five hundred guineas if I could "lick Lady Lucy into shape," and if Lady Mary could be steered to the altar, it was hinted there might be a bonus in it as well. This crew made my cousin Lady Deborah look a positive beauty. I declined firmly, for I had already four other applications waiting, and was sure one of them would be more to my liking. Mrs. Crewe sat in silent astonishment as I allowed one grande dame after another to enter my sitting room to be interviewed.

"One would think it was *you* who was doing the hiring, Olivia," she quizzed me, when we were alone later.

"It pays to advertise," I told her, smiling at the folly of society. It was plain I had become a new rage, the more desirable for being expensive and unique. There was only one Miss Fenwick to go around, and each mama was determined to have me. You would not believe the perquisites I was offered—a suite of my own—that was already set on by myself, but that was only the beginning of it. It was known after the first interview that I had my own carriage. I was offered free stabling as a matter of course, but Lady Norton threw in a free groom as well. Lady Correy offered me my own box at the opera for the season, while a Mrs. Johnson (an honorable Mrs. Johnson actually) would provide a personal maid, no less. All this without their having any clear idea what *I* was to provide! They didn't really care. I would provide an item for them to brag about to their friends. I was a new and rare muslin, my price bruited about town, and hiring me would tell their friends they could afford anything. A sad comment on humankind really, but there you are. If any foolish thing were limited and its price shot to the skies, they would each vie for it.

Mrs. Crewe and I dined in the fashionable dining hall of the Pulteney each day. Not a private parlor—it was not necessary to guard against any undesirable element at the Pulteney. Part of the glamour of residing there was the company one rubbed shoulders with at dinner and tea. I often heard myself discussed.

"Do you suppose that is her?" I heard one eager lady ask, having at the time no idea it was myself she meant. There was an Italian princess being spoken of a great deal.

I looked in the direction the ladies looked and saw an extremely modish creature, draped in furs and plastered with expensive jewelry. She held a pug dog, which she handed to a black page who taggled at her heels. "The Italian princess, probably," I said to Mrs. Crewe.

"I didn't hear she had a dog," one of the ladies said. "Surely a governess would not have a black page."

Mrs. Crewe looked at me and smiled. "Don't let it put ideas in your head," she said.

"No, no. Bringing my team with me is enough. I draw the line at a page."

"Mrs. Johnson says her gowns are all of French design," the more talkative of the misinformed pair went on. I looked down at my dark green serge suit, rather a plain suit really, and shook my head.

"Of course they would be." The other took it up. "Lady Monterne told Lady Glanmore she is the most stylish dresser she ever saw. And Lady Glanmore told Mrs. Norton she has a German princess staying with

17

her, but she is using an alias so as not to embarrass Prinney. One of his *chères amies,* no doubt."

"Shame on you, Mrs. Crewe," I chided her.

"I wish your mama could be here. How she would love it!"

We continued listening to the ladies at the next table. "She sent Mrs. Norton away with a flea in her ear, you must know, and she was willing to go as high as five hundred, to keep her sister from getting the woman. They say she won't even *see* you unless you are at least a countess."

"You'll end up a millionaire after a year in service," Mrs. Crewe said.

"I have already set the price, and do not intend to raise it. This gossiping is getting out of line. To say I would not work for anyone lower than a countess—one would take me for a parvenue."

Mrs. Crewe gave me a very sly look, but I am not a person who is impressed by a title or blue blood. They do not by any means guarantee excellence. They are perhaps an indication of it, no more.

This occurred at dinner on the third day of our stay at the hotel. The next morning, I received another batch of crested letters, and was interviewing again in the afternoon. We went downstairs for tea and more eavesdropping that same afternoon. I was being discussed again, by a man and his wife I presumed, as they sat together.

"I *will* have her, whatever you may say, Phil," the woman stated firmly. Already I had an inkling it was a superior governess they discussed. "Everyone in town is after her. The Duchess told me she is unexceptionable, and you may be sure if she got an earl, soon to be a duke, for that old nag of Monterne's, she can do as well for my Alice."

"Alice does not require a governess to lend her coun-

18

tenance. Her father is an eminent peer, her dowry is twenty-five thousand pounds, and even if her mother is a peagoose, she is bound to make a good match."

I wondered what eminent peer I was listening to, and what peagoose. A peek around the potted palms they use for privacy between tables at the Pulteney showed me no more than a dark blue shoulder. Peering over chair backs, Mrs. Crewe told me the wife wore a high poke bonnet with black ostrich feathers.

"That foolish Nell Johnson thinks to get her by turning a kitchen maid into a personal servant. Widgeon. It is clear the woman is put off by their nonsense. My plan is as follows, Philmot, and I don't want you to say anything to let Miss Fenwick think otherwise. A superior woman of that sort—it is progressive education she is interested in—you see. You know I have always placed a great stress on the importance of education, and I shall tell her so. I'll let her know I expect her to see my gels receive a good, sound, modern schooling, and see if I don't get her."

"I will be surprised if a governess from Bath proves to be an intellectual giant. Miss Silver was plenty good enough for the girls. It was folly to let her leave, with only one year more to go before Dottie is out. You must remember it is Lady Monterne who is passing the verdict. If she has turned blue or even clever it is news to me. The whole family are next door to yahoos."

This slur on my relatives cut as deeply as the one on my own intellectual accomplishments. "Do you suppose that is her?" the woman asked with an awful eagerness, as a portly dame with gray hair waddled into the room. It was amazing what different forms I was imagined to inhabit during that week.

"I cannot think so. Mrs. Norton described her as a youngish woman of somewhat plain appearance," the escort replied dampingly.

I was becoming very peeved with Lady Norton. Plain appearance indeed! I do not call myself a beauty, which is not to say a few others have not done so. I believe I rate a kinder term than plain. Stylish at least; attractive perhaps, if one is very nice in his notions of feminine beauty. My eyes are gray, my nose straight, my teeth all present and all of the proper color. My hair is not, alas, sable or chestnut, but a decent darkish brown. I have been called an elegant female by my worst enemy (Mrs. Bricker, whose husband favors me for an occasional fit of gallantry, hence the enmity). Yes, I think Mrs. Norton was vengeful to call me plain.

"Cora, my dear," a newcomer gurgled, approaching the woman in the high poke. "Have you seen it in the *Herald?* A paragraph in the society column about that Miss Fenwick you are after."

I heard the paper being snatched from fingers, heard, or imagined, a puffing of excitement as the paragraph was read, and was seized of a sudden with a similar eagerness myself. "Let us go, Mrs. Crewe, and see what nonsense they are writing up in the *Herald,*" I suggested. As we left, I heard the husband being sent off to pick up a *Herald,* complaining all the way, but going just the same, like a dutiful, henpecked spouse. He looked rather well from behind. A pity he had sunk into a delivery boy for a cantankerous and foolish wife.

I could write a whole book about that week of interviews. What an education it was! Women willing to lie, cheat, tear up their friends and relatives behind their backs, pay any sum on earth for the services of an unknown governess from Bath, only because she had had the impertinence to advertise in a large black-edged box in the papers, and to put up at the Pulteney to discuss possible employment. They couldn't have cared less whether I could speak or write a word of English or any other language, or teach their daughters anything. They wanted me because everyone else wanted me. But enough. I eventually bestowed the crown of my expensive services on Lady Synge, that same woman who wore the high poke bonnet and black ostrich feathers. She was not so bad as the others, but, of more importance, I did not dislike her daughters. She had two of them, the right number, and of the right ages. The elder, named Alice, was being presented right away, and it was really the younger I was in charge of. Lady Synge inferred that Alice's spare time would also be devoted to me, in the hope that I could, even at this late stage, add some little patina to her polish. The younger would be presented in one year, which suited me. One year with the Synges would lend my life some regularity, without letting it sink into monotony.

Before positively settling on Lady Synge, I wished to meet the girls. She offered to bring them to me, but I was desirous as well to view her home, and offered to drive over to Russell Square. I would have preferred Grosvenor or Cavendish, but Russell Square was close to the Museum, which institution is sadly overlooked as an educational resource. The Harleian and Cottonian libraries so very interesting! Lady Synge's mansion was acceptable. Its decor within was more flamboyant than appealed to me, but the chambers set aside for my use were unexceptionable, a good bedroom and a small but comfortable sitting room ensuite, to which she agreed to add a desk and some extra lamps for night work. Of more importance than these material details, of course, were the girls.

Miss Crowell, the elder, was the less attractive of the two. Neither one was what one would call an Incomparable. Both had brownish-red hair and hazel eyes. Miss Crowell was taller and thinner; Miss Dorothy had a fuller face, still with something almost of baby fat clinging to her body and cheeks. She had dimples and a winning smile. I liked her at once, but was careful not to be overly friendly, as I felt a stiffer demeanor would yield better results in the lessons. Their papa was only a baron, which is why I call them Miss Crowell and Miss Dorothy. Despite what was said of me at the Pulteney, you see, I was willing to work for someone lower than a countess.

A fairly minor point arises, but one that will save confusion later if I mention it now. The blue shoulder sitting with Lady Synge in the dining room at the Pulteney turned out to be not her husband after all, but her brother. Her husband, Lord Synge, whom I met briefly, had no shoulders. He had a very large stomach, held up by a pair of long, thin and unshapely shanks, giving somewhat the illusion of a stomach walking on stilts. He had graying blond hair, blue eyes and the air of a surprised ostrich on his little face. Not one of the more charming examples of our "eminent peers." He was a man it would be easy to forget were it not for his odd appearance. His wife found him easy to forget despite it. She had grown accustomed to his physical oddities, one concludes. I found it hard to do so.

Once I had decided to accept the position, I was eager to get out of the hotel. You would gape to hear what I paid there each day, though of course I paid the bill for Mrs. Crewe as well. She denied herself nothing the establishment offered. A constant stream of footmen wended their way to our door, bearing assorted drinks, newspapers, and so on. Her relatives were very kind to us. Besides helping me select my tilbury and team, they kept it for me till I required it. I sent around for it, and was soon on my way to Russell Square, while Mrs. Crewe went on to her relatives.

I was a little wary of driving in London, not so much due to the heavier traffic than we get at home, as to the speed practiced. One would think they were all participating in a race. The team I had got were biddable, however, and the tilbury a neat, manageable affair. It was a light carriage, open you know, with only two wheels, but done up in the first style of elegance—a deep blue with some gilt trim which I personally would have omitted as being slightly ostentatious, though I have seen more garish ones in the streets since, driven by ladies of the first stare. The greatest advantage to my rig was being able to do without a groom. A street boy was always happy to hold the reins for a penny if I wished to descend and go into a few shops. While it lacked the dash of a high perch phaeton, it was plenty dashing enough for a governess. Not unlike the rig driven by Lady Alton, the Duchess of Tavistock's middle daughter.

My tilbury was taken round to the mews, and I entered the portals of Synge House to take up my new life.

Chapter Three

LADY SYNGE—I HAVE not yet told you much about her, if I recall aright. She was a noisy jay, to strike a comparison that would match her up with her ostrich of a husband. Noisy, bold, self-seeking, predatory—all the unpleasant characteristics we associate with the jay, and some of its fine feathers as well, to draw the attention of bird lovers and fanciers of fine feathers. She was dark haired, a rather handsome woman, full figured, as ladies in the shade of forty are apt to be if they don't watch the sweet tray. Lady Synge watched it closely enough, but only to select those choice morsels to add to her avoirdupois.

She came swooping down on me as soon as I was announced, to carry me off to the saloon to meet a brace of fellow jays I could hear squawking in the next room. As we are all being birds this chapter, I shall dub myself the *rara avis*. The others sat regarding me with popeyed curiosity, waiting to hear what words of wisdom would fall from my four hundred guinea mouth. I scanned my mind for something worthy of their wait.

All I could think of was Indian muslin, which was singularly inappropriate amidst this silken bower of gowns. I professed myself delighted to make their acquaintance, very happy with London, and when queried for the health of Lady Monterne, I replied she enjoyed excellent health when I had left her a few weeks ago. Having come in anticipation of being outraged, they were not happy with this bland civility —who shall blame them? Lady Synge was even less pleased, and urged me on to expatiate on my views on progressive education.

I was arrogant and outrageous enough on that subject to give them some tales to carry on to their next gathering. "I hope to do my little bit to mitigate the awful ignorance of the next generation of ladies who will rule London," I told them. This was more like it! Lady Synge beamed on me, her chest puffing up with pride.

"How do you propose to accomplish that, Miss Fenwick?" one of her guests asked.

"By avoiding the errors of their elders. I shall discourage them from wasting whole afternoons in idle gossip." I then arose, exclaiming, "Nor is the body to be forgotten in a lady's training. I hope my charges are not hanging over a book or tea table in such fine weather, Lady Synge?" Just a little disparaging look at the plate of cream buns, which I had declined to partake of, at this juncture.

"We shall look into it at once," she replied, hopping up to accompany me abovestairs herself, while two countesses, a baronet's lady and the wife of an M.P. sat waiting. Her face was positively glowing with gratification, and though I could not see the other faces, I could hear the exalted chirpings as we left.

The Crowell girls were doing precisely what I expected they would be, and that, on a really fine afternoon in

April, the best weather of the year for going out. They sat curled up, Miss Crowell on a bed reading a book that bore a suspicious marble cover (the hallmark of trashy gothic novels, if you are too high in your literary tastes to be aware of it), Miss Dorothy nominally on a chair, though three-quarters of her body was off it, with her legs stuck out straight in front of her, like a tired old ecclesiastic after a hard day's preaching. Dr. Eberhard used to assume that very pose in the privacy of his study, where Papa and I occasionally have found him in the past.

They leapt to attention when we entered, upon receipt of an admonishing glance and whooshing sound from their mama. They made a passable curtsey, looking at me with some trepidation. It occurred to me for the first time to wonder what they thought of me. The opinion of society I had a fair idea of, but it was these two young ladies I would have to deal with on a day to day basis, and the looks exchanged between them gave me the idea they were not at all happy to be blessed (or cursed) with having got me. This little latent hostility must be done away with at once. It was for this reason I ignored the lazy and time-wasting manner in which they had been passing the afternoon.

"I would not dream of keeping you from your company a moment longer, Ma'am," I told her firmly. "What *will* they think of me, causing you to treat them so shabbily?" She was swift enough to recognize a mild rebuke in this misplacing of blame, and left, very happy to have this saucy speech to relate below. She had not paid four hundred guineas for a governess who behaved herself.

At last I was alone with my charges, to come to terms with them. They both eyed me, frightened, standing at attention, waiting for the terrible rare bird to crow, or chirp, or bite. "Well, ladies," I said in my heartiest voice, "What a beautiful day it is." This banality was not sufficient to rouse them to speech. I stifled the impulse to remind them it is one's social duty to reply to any effort at communication. An offer of a seat would not have been out of place either. I indirectly brought this solecism to their attention. "Shall we be seated, and set about getting to know each other?" I asked. Still no reply. I sat down in the established mode of a lady, with my back straight, my arms folded in my lap, and said no more till they had each found a chair. When the youngest daughter resumed her lounge, I just kept looking with my brows raised in silent rebuke till she assumed a more decent posture.

Though Dorothy was the younger, she was the first to find her tongue. "What are you going to teach us?" she asked, with some interest.

"A good question. First I must discover what it is you already know," I answered.

"Alice knows everything," she informed me, then snickered into her fingers in a way that called to mind Doris. Seeing my brow darken, she withdrew the fingers.

"How nice for Miss Crowell," I said, with a slightly chilly smile meant to indicate my surprise at this singular accomplishment in one so young. "It is she who ought to be the instructress, is it not?"

"She is no longer in the schoolroom is all I meant," Dorothy explained.

"We are not running a schoolroom precisely," I said, knowing well a young lady would strongly resent being put back behind a desk when she thought she had left it forever. Her presence told me Lady Synge intended to maximize her yield on the investment by including Alice as much as possible.

"What do you mean?" Miss Crowell asked, with a faint dawning of interest.

"Why, I am sure ladies of your age (ladies under

27

twenty are so happy to be thought older!) are more than familiar with French, geography and needlework —the work of *young* girls. We shall push on to give you a little knowledge that will set you apart from the common run."

"I hope you are not going to teach us Latin!" Miss Dorothy said. "Uncle Philmot said you would be trying to teach us Latin and Greek."

"How odd! I cannot recall having discussed your curriculum with your Uncle Philmot in the least. Is he a clairvoyant?"

"I don't think so. He is only an earl," Dorothy told me.

There had thus far been no indication Miss Crowell knew a thing after leaving the schoolroom, but she knew I was making a joke at least, and told her sister so. I endeavored to talk to the pair in a serious fashion for some fifteen minutes, but could not make heads or tails of what they had been studying. This I did learn. They could not discourse for two sentences in French on the most mundane of matters. They did not recognize a mention of the Bard of Avon to refer to William Shakespeare. They were unaware the Eternal City referred to Rome, and were none too sure whether our Prime Minister was Lord Liverpool or Lord Castlereagh. That was the depth to which the education of the very flower of Albion's womanhood had sunk. Miss Crowell, in an effort to redeem herself, said a word in praise of Monk Lewis's foolish novel, *The Monk,* and offered to lend it to me after she was finished. This was the tome she perused so keenly when I entered. I told her I had so many important and really worthwhile books to read that I could not spare the time for mere amusement.

"Uncle Philmot recommended it," she told me.

In order to discover just how ignorant the pair were,

I decided to give them a little test of what might be considered the basic knowledge of an adult. Their brows pleated in consternation at the prospect. Must they swot up for it? No indeed, its purpose was to see what they knew without swotting. This cheered them immensely, but I was beginning to form the idea neither of them must pass my test. It was my hope to make them perfectly aware they were savages, to increase (say initiate) a hunger for learning. I took a polite leave, wishing Miss Crowell pleasure of her novel, and dropping Miss Dorothy a hint I had mistaken her for a servant when I had entered to see her sprawling like a slattern. Peeping over my shoulder as I pulled the door closed, I was happy to see Dorothy sitting up and straightening her skirts, while Alice frowned at the cover of her book, then put it aside.

Thence to my own chambers, to see laid out for my delectation two back issues of *La Belle Assemblée* and a box of bonbons. I slid both into the trash bin and busied myself setting up those books I intended using for the girls. Till dinner time I was not disturbed, except for a servant who came to unpack my trunks, Lady Synge come to see if I were comfortable, a man servant sent to enquire whether I would be wanting my carriage that afternoon, and Miss Dorothy (sent by her mama) to ask whether I would care for a cup of tea or a glass of wine. Despite these few interruptions, I was able to set up my test to illustrate to the young ladies, including Miss Crowell, that she was not quite ready to graduate from *my* classroom.

It was not my intention to throw in a free education for Lady Synge, though she was certainly in need of one. When we dined *en famille* that evening with no company at all, it was revealed to me that what thoughts I got into the pates of my charges were the only intelligent ones they were likely to contain. From neither the ostrich nor the jay were they likely to hear anything like an original idea. What was called conversation in the household was nothing else but gossip, and a discussion of future plans for entertainment. One would have no way of knowing that in that year of our Lord, 1817, hundreds of young girls and boys were starving in the gutters. No, what we heard was that Prinney had served a dinner with thirty-six entrées, and four each of soups, fish and *contre-flancs*. No such important matters as the suspension of habeas corpus, the meeting of a select committee to discuss the wretched state of lawlessness in the city and country, nor any of the riots taking place ever arose. The great dissension in their world was understood to be Beau Brummell's falling out with the Prince Regent. That vied for top honors with Princess Charlotte's being possibly enceinte as *the* important doing of the day. Any mention of the riots occurring in the textile industry was turned into a tirade on the botched work of the laundress in washing Dorothy's best mulled jaconet gown, and so it went through two courses and three removes, an unconscionable amount of food, considering the starving masses.

After dinner, Lord and Lady Synge took Miss Crowell to a small rout party, while I remained behind to make a second copy of my test, and to set my room to rights. There is such a deal to do after the convulsion of moving. All one's bits and pieces to be relocated, to find the right spot for the favourite ginger pot, to arrange the desk and lamps to best advantage, to try to locate the letter that requires early answering. These and similar chores took up my evening. I did not entirely neglect Dorothy either. I invited her in to join me after I had achieved some semblance of order, and let her rattle on to give me a better idea what was in her head.

She was an open, artless young thing, likable in

spite of her shocking ignorance. She was also a fund of useful background material. From her I learned Alice was "head over heels" in love with Captain Tierney, an officer in the dragoons. Mama disliked the connection, and had in her eye a certain Lord Harmsworth, whom the sisters agreed was "a stick." Dorothy had not yet succumbed to a passion for anyone in particular. She liked older, dashing bucks, but preferred dogs and horses to men in general. A certain pooch named Toddles in honor of his hobbling gait also joined us. He chewed his way through the toe of one of my blue slippers during the course of the evening, for which stunt he received a slap no harder than a love pat, and a tolerant "Bad doggie!". I paid a guinea for those slippers, but there was no mention of replacing them.

The next morning after breakfast, I herded my two uneager charges into the morning parlor (declining the schoolroom to lend an adult air of playing games to the test). I confess unblushing I could not have passed that test myself without recourse to an encyclopedia. One thinks she knows the longest river, the highest mountain, the most populous city in the country, and a host of other things we all ought to know, but in fact unless we are much inclined to statistics, these useless pieces of trivia elude us. I could see them squirming as they bothered the ends of their pens. If this sounds a nasty stunt to play a couple of harmless girls, I agree with you. It was, but it was done, as I mentioned, to make them aware of their ignorance. Miss Crowell got a score of six out of fifty; Miss Dorothy obtained seven, but when in doubt she guessed, whereas her more cautious sister left a multitude of blanks. They were suitably chastened, and sat without a word of protest after this to discover the forty-four and forty-three answers respectively they had not known.

It was while they were setting to this chore, turned

loose in their papa's library to discover its secrets, that Lady Synge came to pester me for the second time that morning. She had already bothered us once during the test, but I put her off. "All done testing my girls, Miss Fenwick?" she asked, sticking her nose in, and trying pretty hard to follow with her toe.

"Not yet, I'm afraid," I replied firmly, guarding the door.

"I shall tell Lady Bartlett they are busy then," she said, fairly agreeably. When neither of my girls showed the least sorrow at missing out on Lady Bartlett's call, I felt this dame was no favorite with them.

Not more than fifteen minutes passed before she was back a third time, to announce their uncle wished to see them. It was rapidly becoming clear I must establish ground rules, or we would never get a thing accomplished. I suggested that the young ladies limit their visiting hours to the afternoon, if we were to complete the agenda I had set out for the day, which was no more than discovering the answers to the test.

"But it is their Uncle Philmot," she insisted, a little more forcibly than before.

"Has he come a great distance to see them?" I asked, knowing it was not the case. This was undoubtedly Uncle Philmot, the clairvoyant, who had forecast my teaching Latin and Greek.

Dorothy snickered. "All the way from Hanover Square," she answered.

"One dislikes to leave Lord Philmot waiting," the mama essayed. "He would like to meet you as well, Miss Fenwick."

I had no objection to keeping him waiting a millennium, but the truth is, I was wearied to death, and foresaw a glass of wine or a cup of tea, along with an opportunity of informing Lord Philmot his crystal ball must have developed a crack, for his reading of my curriculum was out. "Let us go then, but in future we must be quite firm about the girls' schedule not being interrupted every few minutes," I said severely.

Miss Crowell and her sister were not slow to take advantage of the reprieve. They would have dashed before us to the saloon, had I not got a hand on their elbows and mentioned that age preceded beauty, to give them the lesson in an inoffensive way.

It was Lady Synge and myself who entered the saloon first, with her age in advance of whatever remnants of beauty I possessed. Deduction led me to conclude the tall, elegant gentleman standing in a slouching attitude with his elbow on the mantelpiece was Lord Philmot. There was that in his countenance that set one's back up before he said a word. I knew the words, when he spoke, would not be pleasant. He had what would be called in a boy tow-colored hair, though the texture was not at all coarse like the broken flax. It was sleekly groomed. Sleek is as good a word as any to describe his whole appearance: a very well-tailored jacket, immaculate cravat, striped waistcoat. He was elegantly thin with lean cheeks, a narrow nose, long graceful fingers and a weary, bored expression on his face that one ought not to assume when he goes calling. At least I have been taught one ought to put herself out to be pleasant when in company, and have never been told there existed a different rule for gentlemen.

"Ah here you are, Sis," he said, in a languid way, but his eyes were on myself, and they were full of mischief. The voice I recognized at once as belonging to the blue shoulder that had sat in the dining room at the hotel. That long ago he had been casting slurs on my abilities.

We were made acquainted, the words acknowledged by a bow on his lordship's part, and a minimal curtsey on my own, to match his stiff deportment. Without so much as a word exchanged between us, he turned his attention to his nieces.

"Well, well," he said in a mocking way, "are you girls so full of punctilio already, after one day in Miss Fenwick's care, that you do not greet me with your customary exuberance? What a blessing! I shall be eternally grateful to you, Ma'am, for curbing their enthusiasm. I am usually greeted with wild whoops and a demand for sugarplums. If the toes of my boots escape untrammeled I count myself fortunate."

Still, I felt he disliked the lack of enthusiasm in their greeting. They did no more than curtsey and say good morning, then we were all seated. It was unfortunate Lady Synge immediately took into her head to begin extolling my virtues, including my dislike of being interrupted by callers. "For she is testing the girls, Philmot, just like a college. You would not credit the hard questions she has set up for them."

"Thinking of entering Christ Church next season, are you, Dottie?" he asked, with a sardonic smile.

"They'd never let her in. She only got seven right out of fifty," Miss Crowell told him, with of course a retaliation on the younger girl's part of Alice's mark.

"You pose difficult questions, Ma'am," he told me. "Just what is it you have in mind schooling the ladies for? It is news to me if their mama has other plans for them than marriage, in a year or two."

"Do you not feel it incumbent on a gentleman's wife to have a good education?" I asked, trying to smile politely.

"Good in the sense of being pertinent, certainly," he allowed. "What are these abstruse matters of which you know only twelve percent, Alice?"

"All kinds of things. I had no notion I was so uneducated. I bet you don't know half of them either, Uncle Phil."

"Do you indeed? Are your charges allowed to place a wager, Miss Fenwick?" he asked, with such a supercilious curl to his lip I longed to have his ignorance displayed.

"I see no harm in a family wager, if their mother does not object."

"Fire away," he said to the girls.

"What is the biggest river in England?" Dottie asked. As this was the first question, she would have had the answer looked up long since.

"Do you speak of biggest in drainage-basin and volume discharged, or longest, or widest?"

Dottie looked a question at me. "I meant the longest, naturally," I answered quickly.

"Odd you did not *say* so. Is accuracy considered of no importance in your lessons? Actually, of course, it is an utterly pointless question, the way you meant it. The tributaries must be taken into account as well, and in so many cases the tributary stream itself is another river. I think we must admit that question to be unanswerable. What else, Dottie?"

"The largest island off Britain," she said.

"The largest in land mass, Lord Philmot," I said, with a tinge of sarcasm to show what I thought of his nit-picking. "Not in height or weight or population."

He acknowledged my thrust with a slight inclination of the head. "One of the Outer Hebrides, I should think."

"You're wrong!" Alice crowed. "It is the Isle of Man."

I saw my error at once, but it was too late to rectify it.

"Surely the question said off *Britain*, not England?" he asked, scarcely able to contain his glee. "Unless Miss Fenwick has unilaterally annulled the treaty of 1707 which legislated the union of England and Scotland to form Great Britain, I must take exception to your answer, Alice."

"You may be sure Miss Fenwick said England in her test, Phil," his sister said. "These girls are as ignorant as swans. I don't know where they get it, but she will cure them."

"It seems pointless to continue with these questions," he said in a dismissing way to the girls. "Is that what your lessons consist of, memorizing useless bits of disconnected facts by rote?"

"The lessons have not yet begun," I answered coolly. "This was no more than a little examination to discover what points in the girls' backgrounds want strengthening."

"Make sure you do not omit to teach them the importance of accuracy," he suggested.

After a few such barbed comments, the wine was brought out, and Philmot turned his shoulder on me rather pointedly, to speak to his nieces. "I have a surprise for you," he announced. Clamorous shouts, very loud, very unladylike, poured forth. He was the playful sort of uncle who had to tease them for five minutes before revealing the great treat. "I have decided to take you to Richmond Hill tomorrow," he told them.

This, I must say, did not sound like much of a treat to me. The view from the hill of seven counties and Windsor Castle is a fine prospect certainly, but it cannot have been an entirely novel one for ladies who spent considerable time in London each year. There had to be more to the treat than this. It was from the exuberant Dottie that I got an inkling of it. "You have got our mounts sent up!" she exclaimed.

It turned out he had been training a pair of hacks for his nieces at his estate, and they were to be sent to town, arriving that same day. I do not ride much, and never could get excited about that unpleasant form of exercise, though it is close to a national mania. If one has a short distance to traverse, one's legs are good enough; if long, a carriage is better. After a deal of excited babble, I said, "It will be a pleasant jaunt for you, after your morning at studies."

"We plan to leave in the morning and make a day of it," Lord Philmot said, with a challenging look at me. His sister had been at pains to inform him the mornings were to be uninterrupted. He did it on purpose to vex me. I could not understand why he had taken such a violent dislike to me, even in advance of having met me.

The three Synge ladies looked to me, Lady Synge quite simply frightened, Miss Crowell uncertain but not unhopeful, Dorothy pleading with her puppy eyes. "It is not a great distance. You can go and return in an afternoon," I pointed out in a reasonable manner.

"I have planned a picnic. Even now my cook is roasting fowl and preparing food for it," he replied. After staring hard at me, he looked to his sister, "Well, Sis, what do you say? Can the girls come?" he asked.

It was all arranged the mornings were mine, and to avoid coming to cuffs with me, Lady Synge said, "That is up to Miss Fenwick," in an effort to dump the problem in my lap.

"Have you abrogated your parentship of your daughters, entrusting it entirely to a stranger?" he asked in a thin voice. "*You* are their mother. It is for you to decide what they may do."

"But Miss Fenwick . . ." she began, looking at me with eyes that pleaded for help.

"The mornings have been reserved for serious work," I pointed out. Dottie's puppy eyes were on the verge of tears. To settle the unpleasant matter, I went on, "However, as you have set your cook to prepare a picnic without first ascertaining whether your guests are available, Lord Philmot, let them by all means go with you *this time*."

"My cook and other *servants* are not the people of prime concern in *my* household," he answered, as much as though to say they (meaning I) were in *this* household.

A servant was precisely what I did not consider myself, nor intend anyone else to consider me either. While I thought of the most cutting reply I could decently make, I was prevented from any speech by the violent vocal outpourings of the girls, and a very relieved "Then it is all settled!" from their mama.

Lord Philmot did not long remain with us. It was back to the library with the students, where we remained, they ascertaining various authors, countries and historical personages, while I scrutinized the test for further inaccuracies, without finding one! I was extremely vexed that my two vaguely worded questions should have been the very ones brought to his attention. After lunch, I took the girls to the museum to study Sir Hans Sloan's collection of artworks. The natural history section must wait for another day.

Chapter Four

WE LOST A WHOLE day while my girls dawdled along to Richmond Hill, and an evening in their relating to me the fine time they had enjoyed, the pleasure in no small part being due to the amusing sayings of Uncle Philmot and his friend, a Miss Peters. Dottie informed me, with no prodding and very little display of interest on my part, that this Miss Peters was an Incomparable in the class of Venus at least. She was said to be the latest in a long line of Incomparables who had enjoyed the uncle's favor. A second day was not to be similarly wasted. We discussed French drama in the morning, with a few scenes from Racine read aloud by us, each taking a character. *Andromaque* it was, a favorite of mine, though many prefer *Phèdre*. There is nothing like the pure, classical lines of Racine and Corneille to improve one's French pronunciation. Delightful, but the girls found it a little heavy going, and in the afternoon I agreed to take them to Somerset House in my tilbury to see the display of French paintings on view, which were a sort of peace offering from the French government after the havoc created by that upstart, Bonaparte.

David, the Guillotine artist, enjoyed a considerable vogue with the ladies. I preferred the work of the more modern Ingres myself—beautiful the skin tones he does, and with less of the cold formality of David. We spent the next week studying French culture—literature, art, a dab of history of the recent past. I cured Dottie of the habit of calling the French Revolution the French Resolution, and accustomed them both to the roles of Robespierre, Louis XVI, Marie Antoinette, and the rabble in that unfortunate squabble. They displayed a shocking ignorance. The depths of it could still astound me after a week's exposure. But what can one expect? Their mama's only comment on the era—an era she had lived through (and not as a child either) was that the English fashions had been very dull at the time, with no Gallic style to copy.

I managed to curtail social visits rather effectively that week. *No* morning callers, though Alice generally left us in the afternoon to attend some function or other. Dottie also escaped on a few afternoons. Once she went to Hyde Park with Miss Peters and Alice. They insisted on telling me all about it.

"I suppose your uncle was along?" was all I asked, then was obliged to hear not only that he was there, but every word that left his mouth.

"He asked us how the Latin and Greek lessons were coming along," Dottie finished up.

"I hope you told him it is French we are studying!"

"I did, and he thinks you are very brave to tackle Racine with us. When are we going to finish *Andromaque,* Miss Fenwick?"

"Finish it? You cannot mean we did not finish it! I have read it so often I have it by heart. I forgot we had not done so."

40

"No, we only read the first act, then you said we were tired."

"We shall finish it tomorrow. What else had Lord Philmot to find a fault with?"

"He was mostly flirting with Miss Peters. She is very pretty," Alice told me.

Let me assure you I am not so shallow as to think one can learn anything useful about a foreign country in a week, but after one week on France, I decided it was time to vary our studies. We turned next to the English arts. My own preference must arise here. Literature and painting were the main areas we dealt with, though history was by no means neglected. We studied *Romeo and Juliet,* which I thought might be a light introduction to the works of Shakespeare. I intended following it up later with something more demanding—*Hamlet* or *Lear* perhaps. From Shakespeare we proceeded to more modern times, omitting, alas, those interesting Restoration Comedies that are unfit for young ears. A pity, really. No matter, Sheridan retains something of the light touch and wit of Wycherley and Etherington in his *School for Scandal* and *The Rivals,* and despite the naughty name of the former, it is not at all objectionable. The latter has a good lesson on the matter of deception. It was of particular interest to me as it was set in my home town of Bath. We read *The Rivals* together, doing some vocabulary study to explain painstakingly each joke to issue from that wonderful harpy, Mrs. Malaprop. A second reason for choosing that particular play was that it was to be put on at Covent Garden that season, one of their first showings.

My understanding with Lady Synge was that I was to be treated quite as family, attending the large social functions, though I retained the option of dining alone when she held intimate parties of a family nature. Her family (and I do not exclude her brother) were all as dull as herself. Once a week she invited cousins, aunts, uncles and so on to her table. I was better entertained with a book and a tray in my room. What had not been worked out was whether I was to make any use of her box at the theater. She had invited me once, but I declined that time, and went to spend an evening with an old friend from Bath, Miss Lacey. If one stayed home every evening, she would sooner or later become responsible for the girls' evenings as well as their days. We were all to attend *The Rivals* together at least.

I had been at Russell Square for two weeks when Lord Philmot made his second intrusion upon my time. As he came in the afternoon, I had no objection to giving his nieces a half hour to visit with him. As I had not been asked to join them in the saloon, I did not do so. I remained behind, continuing my own study and enjoyment of *The Rivals*, which still retained, after more than forty years, the bright luster of a great work. R.B. Sheridan was just recently dead too—how young he must have been when he wrote it. Twenty minutes had elapsed before I heard the sound of feet and voices outside the door, the voices those of the girls, but the tread including a heavier step as well.

"Miss Fenwick, may we go, please?" Dottie chirped, before she was halfway into the room. Miss Crowell came along at a statelier pace beside her uncle. Now that she was out, she was more eager to improve her manners.

"Yes, certainly you may leave, as your uncle has delayed his outing till the afternoon," I answered, with a civil nod to Philmot, who bowed with equal civility (and not a jot more).

"It's not today. It's tonight," Miss Crowell told me. "My uncle wishes to take us to the play, *The Rivals*, that we have been studying all week."

"Two days!" I corrected her swiftly. "But you were to

42

attend *The Rivals* with me, girls," I reminded them, seeing my excuse to go along with Lady Synge and her party vanish before my eyes. "Tomorrow night we are to go." I felt such a surge of annoyance with their uncle I could hardly control it. He might give a little more notice of his parties!

"I would not dream of intruding a second time on Miss Fenwick's plans," he said at once. The nieces both showed long faces at this delay in their outing.

"*I'd* rather go tonight," Dottie said at once. She always said what was in her mind. It was at one time her charm and her fault.

"Your mama has already arranged a party," I pointed out. "Young ladies do not alter their social commitments without a good reason."

"It's only Papa and Cousin Rachel who make up the party," Alice reminded me.

"Uncle Phil hardly ever takes us out in the *evening*," Dottie profferred as a good reason. "In fact, he *never* took me before at night. He has had a tiff with Miss Peters, and so has offered to escort *us*. We are not doing anything tonight."

"As you are free, I shall take you somewhere else," he said.

There turned out to be nowhere else in the whole city he could take them both but to a theater. Dottie was not allowed at routs or balls, but like any young lady-in-training for her debut, she was occasionally allowed at the theater with a relative. Drury Lane popped into my head.

"We could try the Haymarket," Philmot suggested.

"The Haymarket!" I exclaimed with interest, thinking he meant the Opera House. I envisaged something by Handel as suitable for my charges.

"*The Provok'd Wife* is playing at the Haymarket Theater," he went on.

I stared in dismay. The Haymarket Theater was a step down from Covent Garden or Drury Lane, and a Vanbrugh comedy several steps down from Sheridan.

"I cannot think that a suitable play for young ladies," I said.

"Are you familiar with it?" he asked.

"I have not read it. Vanbrugh, however, is not generally considered to have such merit."

"My friends who have attended found it to have considerable merit," he informed me, in a very toplofty manner. He had a face one wished to slap, with no provocation whatsoever.

"You would know what your friends' opinion is worth," I answered. The only friends of Lord Philmot's I had ever heard of were Miss Peters and his relatives, and what I had heard of the former did not incline me to credit her with any more discrimination than the Synges.

"Society usually considers the opinion of Mrs. Burney and Mr. Coleridge worth listening to, particularly on literary matters," he told me, with a dismissing look. "You have heard of Miss Burney, I assume?"

It is impossible to live in England without having heard of our foremost female novelist. Coleridge, of course, was widely known as well to anyone who reads, though he is not my own favorite poet. "When I wish to pass an idle hour, I have often dipped into the works of Miss Burney," I admitted. "Not so edifying as Hannah More, of course, but perfectly harmless."

"With such lukewarm enthusiasm on your part, I hesitate to ask you to join us, Ma'am."

You could have knocked me over with a breath. I had no notion *I* was to be included in the outing. I had come to the city to broaden my circle of friends, and while Philmot was not and never would make a compatible or sympathetic friend for me, he was of all those I knew the most likely to introduce me to a select crowd.

Fanny Burney even! I had said little in praise of her, but she was indeed one of my most favored writers. He regarded me closely while all this was considered. Some aspect on that sardonic face gave me the idea he was reading my mind. This being the case, I expressed a polite disinterest in joining him.

"Pity," was all he said. I was disproportionately let down, to have my refusal accepted so readily.

"What will you do instead?" Dottie asked me.

"I shall find something," I assured her, showing none of the turmoil, the bitter recrimination that was already nagging at me. "Read a book, or write some letters . . ."

"If it is only getting in the evening you intend doing, I suggest you would be better amused at the play," Philmot was kind enough to urge.

I didn't think he would press harder. "Perhaps you're right," I said with no eagerness, but a fine careless lack of interest. "It might be of interest to see what others enjoy."

"Others than whom?" he enquired.

"Others than myself."

"I had not realized Miss Fenwick was a breed apart," he replied, in a tone not far removed from a jeer. I was too relieved to call him to account. "I shall call for you at 8:00."

As soon as we had expressed our approval, he was off. The girls were too excited to return to work after the visit. As their interest was to select the most attractive gown for the outing, I let them go to it. I did not plan to appear as a dowd myself, but as my attendance was in the nature of a chaperone for the girls, I could not don quite what I wished either. I had not attended any London do's for over five years, and was not sure what degree of extravagance the Haymarket Theater called for. Not so grand as Drury Lane or

Covent Garden, I thought. Dottie was still wearing gowns cut high to the neck, and the very simplest of jewelry. It was only from Alice's outfit I could hope for a clue. She had selected a very plain white gown, and her hair too she wore simply dressed. Fancy frills then would be out of place, I thought.

After dinner, I went to my room to prepare myself, wearing a perfectly simple but well designed dark green gown, cut a little low at the neck, but with my shoulders covered. My hair I wore in its customary fashion. A real party would be time enough to alter it to a more stylish mode.

It was clear when Philmot called for us he was surprised at my appearance. Why this should be was not immediately clear. Were the pair of plumes in my hair too ornate for a chaperone? They were short and simple, not towering plumes by any means, but a discreet set of white ostrich feathers that more closely resembled puffs for applying powder than plumes. I then took the notion it was Alice's toilette that displeased him. The surprise, you see, was not of the pleasant sort. The chiseled nose turned down in distaste. I don't know why folks say anyone turned his nose *up* at anything. In displeasure, the nose generally turns down.

He turned his gaze to Alice. "Determined not to be taken for a lady of fashion, I see," was his compliment to her. I felt it might equally apply to myself. I had not realized Alice planned to enliven her appearance with an extremely elegant cape, lined in sable. She looked very fashionable indeed to me.

"I think she looks particularly well," I was impelled to defend, as she had consulted with me on the gown.

"Well enough for a deb, I suppose," he admitted, his eyes flickering from her to me. I had not the excuse of being a deb, and was made to feel it.

We left, with already a little pall over the party, which was quickly driven away by the effervescent Dottie. The two girls sat on one banquette, with Philmot, the last to enter, sitting beside me, but I attached no importance to his having told Dottie to sit with her sister. He attempted a few remarks bordering on the flirtatious, which I was at pains to misunderstand. As soon as we entered the theater, I saw how far I had musjudged in the matter of toilette. The Haymarket's not being one of the liscensed theaters led me to believe it was a sort of second-rate place. Its offerings were not of the first jet, but in the elegance, the positive grandeur of the patrons, there was nothing second-rate about it. There was the glitter of diamonds and precious stones everywhere. My little pair of ostrich plumes shrank to insignificance in the midst of so much finery. No fear of being overdressed! *Au contraire.* I never felt so very like a country bumpkin. I wished I had worn Mama's diamond necklace.

When the asceticism of one's outfit puts her at a disadvantage, the only recourse is to be above such paltry considerations. I must take high ground, adopt a lofty, intellectual tone. In short, I was determined to look down my nose at the play, that I might similarly denigrate those present who took any pleasure in it. I think I might have succeeded, too, had it not been for Dottie.

I managed a pretty quelling stare on the first guffaw Lord Philmot emitted. Though he pretended to ignore it, his second outburst was less raucous, while the rest of the audience greeted the joke more loudly. Throughout the first act, I evinced not the least amusement. I kept my control while Sir John Brute was revealed as a cowardly churl, and the actor playing the role was extremely comical too. It was during the next act, when Sir John entered disguised in a lady's gown, that

47

I had some trouble controlling my mirth. I cannot think why it struck me as funny, for in general I find it not at all amusing to see men wearing ladies' wigs and skirts, and mincing about the stage in a manner that is supposed to imitate a lady, though it is without exception grossly overdone. There seemed to be some contagion in the air that night. Between Philmot's enthusiastic male belly laugh, the girlish giggles of the sisters, the whole audience fairly bellowing, it was too hard to remain indifferent. By the end of the second act, I was in stitches, like everyone else.

It was a heady taste of social life such as I had not had since my own abbreviated season, so long ago. Several pairs of opera glasses were turned toward our box, and at intermission, several of the users of those glasses came in person to meet us. Philmot introduced me only as Miss Fenwick, a friend, but I was quick enough to add my true role in the party.

Many of the playgoers were off to dinners and routs after the performance, but with Dottie along to curb our style, we had to go straight home. The Synges were out, which led me to believe Philmot would leave us at the door. It was not the case. He said, "It is early yet. We oldsters shall have a nightcap, shall we, Miss Fenwick, while the youngsters retire? I am curious to hear your opinion of Vanbrugh, now that you have seen his work performed."

Dorothy stifled a yawn and went toward the stairs, while Alice, feeling herself an oldster, walked toward the saloon. "Goodnight Alice. I hope you enjoyed the play," Philmot said. She took the hint and went after her sister.

I disliked to impose on Lady Synge's hospitality to entertain a gentleman during her absence, but her own brother after all, and at his insistence, not mine. "Sis will not mind," he said, correctly interpreting my hesitation. "I run tame here, and it is not as though you were entertaining a suitor after all."

"No, certainly not!" I answered swiftly, causing a fleeting smile to cross his lips, which looked always on the verge of smiling that evening.

"So, what have you to say of Vanbrugh?" he asked, pouring two glasses of wine.

"It was mildly amusing—well acted."

"I look forward to seeing you when you are more than mildly amused. Do you know, I think it will be actually unladylike, if your roars this evening are any indication."

"You will not find my behavior at any time to be less than ladylike, I hope."

This set him in his place, or seemed to. The hovering smile dwindled noticeably. "How do the lessons go on?" he asked.

I mentioned the French week we had just passed. "And this week you have progressed to England," he confirmed, when I mentioned it. "It will be Italy next week, I expect? Seven days to study a recorded history of twenty-one centuries—that would be three hundred years a day. I think even you, Miss Fenwick, will find yourself a trifle rushed."

"I do not claim to be giving an in depth study of the civilizations of the various countries. An introduction merely. A little glance at the art, literature, and so on."

"What do you construe to be the high points of French culture?" he asked, settling back with his old haughty expression beginning to creep over his face.

I mentioned briefly what we had been doing, which set him to the task of finding fault with it. "I should have thought Voltaire and Rousseau more useful literary vehicles than Racine, if it is the execution of their monarchs you have chosen to select as the apogee of a civilization that led western culture for centuries. I would have called it the nadir myself."

"I did not call it the apogee, sir, merely the climax. Neither did we study Racine in connection with the Revolution. Two separate aspects of French culture, you see, is what we are talking about. History and literature," I stated quickly, smarting under his sarcasm.

"Would it not be more plausible to bring them together, as it was a taste of civilization you mentioned trying to inculcate in the girls? Literature is usually considered to represent the progress of a nation. Odd you chose a seventeenth-century dramatist, who reworked themes from the classical Greek."

"It is not considered odd that we study Shakespeare to familiarize ourselves with English literature; the truly great writers in any language deal with eternal themes and problems. Unlike a second-rate hack such as Vanbrugh."

"How can you say so, Ma'am? A provoked wife is surely as old as the story of creation. I daresay Eve herself was provoked upon occasion. What else is on the girls' curriculum?"

"It is my intention to cut the course to fit the girls' needs. Where I find their knowledge to be lacking, I shall endeavor to strengthen it."

"You will find no lack of areas requiring strengthening," he replied in a sardonic way, but as I thought the slur in this case was on his nieces, I felt no need to object. I soon saw my error. "Manners, for instance. I notice neither of the girls bothered to thank me for having taken them. I thought you would mention it to them."

"I feel it is kinder to draw their lapses to their attention in private," I answered.

"Kinder, but less effective I fancy. You consider

yourself capable to enlighten them in *any* sphere, do you?"

"In those spheres generally considered to be essential in the polite conduct of a young lady I do, yes."

"The world would turn more smoothly if young ladies had less lessons in drama—they have such a natural bent for that, you know—and more in managing a household. They will not be lecturers when they are grown up, but wives."

"I shan't omit more practical matters by any means." I had no idea of teaching them how to run a house actually, but in the areas of health and physical exercise I was quite a fanatic.

"I would be interested to hear what your particular qualifications are in that line, Ma'am."

"I kept house for my father for several years in Bath. I am familiar with domestic management."

"One wonders how efficacious your experience in running a small Deanery will be in instructing ladies who will have to see to the housekeeping of a castle, if they marry well."

"My employers have not seen fit to question my expertise," I reminded him sharply.

"Very true. It does not seem to have occurred to *anyone* to question it."

"It has obviously occurred to *you*."

"When a perfectly capable governess was let go to hire a new one whose qualifications had been so ill explained, I thought it worth a question. If you prove to be *half* as capable as you claim to be, I shall consider my sister to have got a bargain. Even at four hundred guineas," he added.

"You must be sure to ask her after a year is up whether she is satisfied."

"Do you know, I don't think it will take that long," he

answered, with a challenging look. He might as well have said "Fraud." It was inherent in that look.

I thanked him very civilly for a delightful evening, and with my fingers covering a simulated yawn, took my leave of him.

"We shall meet again soon, Miss Fenwick," he warned.

I went straight upstairs and scolded the girls for not having thanked their uncle for his treat. Then I went to my own room to consider his parting shot. He had some influence with his sister; he might make life difficult for me if he took it into his head to do it. I disliked very much the imputation that I would not know how to hold house on a grand scale, but the fact was, he was correct. I had used the words "inclusive education" in my advertisement, along with such phrases as "a progressive education, both practical and academic." They were vague enough to mean anything, though I certainly had not meant them to imply kitchen management. If that was what was expected, however, I would throw it in.

Next morning, I went to the housekeeper. With a little judicious flattery, I contrived to bring her into my camp. She was to teach the teacher. She loved it, especially when I called her my "Instructress." She did not despise the guinea I slipped into her fingers either.

Chapter Five

I MADE SOME SHOCKING (not to say revolting) discoveries in my foray into the kitchen and pantries of Synge House. I hardly know whether it was the waste or the filth that dismayed me most. Our meals were cooked in vessels that must have been excavated from the site of Roman ruins. The housekeeper, Mrs. Ledwell, had never heard of Count Rumford, the philosopher-sage of kitchen management. I, who professed to no particular knowledge, knew at least that milk left standing overnight in a jug will sour. A fool could see it was unnecessary to peel an inch of flesh from potatoes and carrots, and throw half the food into the garbage. But such waste was everywhere evident in the kitchen. A leg of mutton was bought and cooked for a handful of people, with the part not eaten shoved into the pantry to moulder, and attract rats.

I gently suggested to Mrs. Ledwell that she get the kitchen girls to scrub out the pantry shelves with carbolic soap, and scrape the rust from the sauce pans before Cook used them for our dinner. You could scarcely see daylight through the holes of the colander, so clogged was it with congealed matter.

"It's the grease splattering from the roasts that destroys all my things," Cook explained, but with a shamed face that tacitly admitted a brush and soap would have undone much of the stove's work.

"In that case, you ought to see about getting a Bodley Range," I told her. "It has a closed top at least, and the flue on the three sides of the oven gives a good even heat. No wonder our meat is black on the bottom half the time."

"They don't seem to mind, Miss. I've never had no complaints."

"You are getting a complaint now," I pointed out, but to Cook, not my "Instructress," Mrs. Ledwell, whose good offices I required to examine her accounts.

Like the rest of the domestic arrangements, they were in a wretched muddle. Nothing bought in bulk, to save money, and no account ever paid in time to avoid interest. I am sure I could have cut the kitchen bills by a third had it been my job to do so, but I did no more than advise and suggest, and at Cook's beseeching, hint Lady Synge into purchasing a Bodley Range.

She thought it was very dear, and had heard from a friend that it was a monstrous user of coal—fifteen scuttles a day. But she liked well enough to brag about it to her callers, once I had talked her around.

Philmot heard about it on his next visit. I chanced to be with Lady Synge rather than in the schoolroom, as we had gone together to make the purchase, and there was a booklet of instructions for its maintenance that was beyond her comprehension. Philmot sat beside us to peer over his sister's shoulder at the diagram.

"That looks like a very large firebox to me," was his comment. "It will eat up a deal of coal."

"You will notice there is also a nice big boiler."

"How the devil is a woman expected to lift out such a huge container?" he asked.

"If she has any sense, I expect she would use a smaller container to ladle out what she needs at one time."

"Miss Fenwick feels it will keep the kitchen much cleaner," Lady Synge explained.

"The fire is still open in front," he pointed out. He hadn't a good word to say for it, and as no opportunity arose to mention my other efforts in the kitchen, he was left with the idea I had caused his sister to waste her money on a toy. I had the satisfaction of knowing it was not the case. My girls had now at their elbows a neat extract of tips and pointers for the effective management of a household, and we could return to our original academic studies.

We wasted no time in analyzing that farcical comedy of Vanbrugh's, but went straight into Shakespeare. *Hamlet* was our next project. No one could take exception to a perusal of our greatest playwright's greatest play. I had read it many times myself, of course, and set the girls to the task of reading it the next morning. I first sat with them, but found myself so often appealed to to explain a word to them—do the work for them in effect—that I soon picked up a newspaper to bury my nose in, to discourage their interruptions. I read with interest that Lord and Lady Strathacona were to have a large ball.

In the afternoon, I decided to make a quick trip over to leave a card at Deborah's home, as she did not seem to have got my note. She and Jack had set up house on a very grand scale on Charles Street, just at the corner of Berkeley Square. I admit to a feeling of gratification at being on the most intimate terms with a lady who would surely be one of the major hostesses of the

Season in London. Miss Dorothy came with me in my tilbury, while Alice went out with her mother.

"Are you really related to the Strathaconas?" Dottie asked, her eyes growing as she surveyed the mansion, which was roughly twice the size of her own home.

"Lady Strathacona is my cousin," I told her.

"I wonder why she never calls on you. I expect she will ask you to her parties. Will you attend, Miss Fenwick?"

"Certainly I shall. But only in the evenings. I am a working lady, and do not intend to shab off on my duties, only because I happen to be on very intimate terms with Lady Strathacona."

There was some sort of a do in progress that same afternoon. I left my card with the butler, but from the corner of my eye I saw the saloon to be full of ladies and gentlemen. I wondered at first that Debbie had not invited me, as it was quite a large do, but of course she knew my position. She would not wish to embarrass me by asking me when she knew I must work. My lessons had made some good impression on her, for prior to them, she was not at all considerate of other people. I might have taken just *one* afternoon off, however, or even brought the girls with me, as it was a musical party in progress, offering some possibility of instruction. The melodious strains of an Italian soprano, accompanied by a pianist, wafted to my ears. The player was not quite so good as the singer. His accompaniment faltered, lagged the singer a little. Debbie never had much of an ear, poor girl. I would mention it when next we met. I was sure she would be in touch with me to help arrange her ball. She was not much of a dab at anything decorative. She would have guests sitting in saddles or waltzing in a barn, if left to her own devices. I would be happy to help her out.

"The Italian tunes are beautiful, are they not?" I

mentioned to Dottie. "So lyrical, light and graceful. There is no mistaking them for anything else. Scarlatti I believe it was."

"I don't know how you have found time to learn so much, Miss Fenwick," Dottie said.

"I never waste a minute, my girl. There is the secret. We shall rush straight home and see if your mama has any of Scarlatti's sonatas for us to play."

"But it was such a fine afternoon, I hoped we might drive to the Park," she said, turning those puppy eyes on me. There was no denying her a little outing on such a lovely day. We took a leisurely drive, filling our lungs with fresh air. Walking would have been better for us, but of course in the Park one dare not abandon her carriage and we would find no boy to hold the reins.

After having a view of the mansion Debbie was occupying and the largeness of her afternoon party, I came to realize her ball would be one of the year's grander affairs. My insignificant toilette of the play would not be repeated. I would order a gown worthy of the occasion, and was happy I had my first quarter's salary in hand to attend to it, as the purchase of the tilbury and team had cleaned out my own savings. There was some little uncertainty as to just how this was to be arranged. A lady in the normal way would have the modiste come to her home, but this point had not been settled between Lady Synge and myself, and I was careful not to encroach in any way, since her brother was always swift to interfere. I opted for the following method. I would select material and pattern, and take them to a modiste for making up, giving her a set of my measurements to obviate the unpleasantness of undressing on her premises for this job.

Dorothy was always happy to spend an hour in the shops. She was delighted to come with me and select material. The afternoon was not without its instructional aspect, as I took the opportunity to explain to her that a very gaudy shot silk plaid was not in the least pretty, as she seemed to think. I patiently outlined that a lady of quality does not dress to gain attention, but once attention wanders in her direction, it remains happily there for a decent interval. Bright colors were not in the best of taste, nor were the more grotesquely dyed feathers at all what could be called elegant. Subdued colors, well-cut gowns of the best materials, discreetly ornamented, were the criteria I tried to impress upon her. I followed my own judgment to purchase a pale mint green material of gros de Naples, and a pattern that would see it made plain on top, to give the show to my mother's diamond necklace. The skirt would be flounced and scalloped round the bottom to fill out my rather slim figure. Tiers of lace would peep from beneath the gathered-up scallops. Somewhere in the city I hoped to procure green slippers with paste buckles, if they cost me my quarter salary. A lady's elegance does not stop at the hem of her gown, especially if she has been told a few times she has a neat ankle, and knows perfectly well she has a dainty foot.

It remained only to discover of Lady Synge whom she considered a very good modiste, and my gown would be got under way in plenty of time for Debbie's ball. A few compliments on a certain cinnamon colored outfit Lady Synge often chose for an evening out put me in possession of the name and address of Madame Vigneault, who kept shop in a smartly got up hole in the wall on a little street between Bond and Swallow, just off Conduit. It was not my intention to take Miss Dorothy to the establishment with me, but to go alone and leave off the patterns and material, striking a bargain as to price with Madame, Getting away from my charge proved difficult, however, as the call must be made during the business hours of the day, when I was busy.

After wasting twenty-four hours trying to find a suitable excuse to leave the house alone, I could not spare another minute, and took Dorothy with me after all. A half hour in a stylish modiste's shop could hardly impair her character inalterably.

Just after luncheon the two of us set out. We saw little of Alice as the season got into full swing. If she were not too tired, she joined us in the mornings, but seldom in the afternoons. "Where do you take little Dottie today, Miss Fenwick?" Lady Synge asked as we went through the hallway to hop into my waiting tilbury. She had a Lady Roberts with her, in front of whom she was eager to show me off.

I could not let her down. "We are accomplishing two projects at one time, Ma'am. Taking advantage of the delightful weather for a drive and later a walk, and doing some study of our London architecture."

My employer nodded her head to Lady Roberts in an "I told you so" sort of way, to indicate how well I was worth my money. "What buildings are you going to see?" she asked. "It will be St. Pauls I suppose, and the Tower."

I knew by this time Lady Synge liked me to be a little more esoteric, especially in front of her friends. "Perish the thought, Ma'am," I replied playfully. "We can do without the monotony of Wren and such well-known landmarks as the Tower. We mean to look around Trafalgar Square—Whitehall, the St. James area. The Old Admiralty building is worth a look. Perhaps we shall sketch Adam's classic portico. The clock tower and archway at the Horse Guards too are rather interesting. The front of Harrington House is a must—one of the finer examples of Queen Anne architecture in the city."

The mama's gratification beamed on us. "Be sure to pay attention to Miss Fenwick," she reminded her daughter. We made our curtseys and hastened out, not before my employer began an exhortation of my many accomplishments.

I was made to feel sufficiently guilty at this little deception that I *did* cruise quickly past the aforementioned spots, pointing out such features as were readily assimilated without stopping, but e'er long I turned my team back north to the establishment of Madame Vigneault.

I guessed as soon as I entered the door that it was not the sort of establishment a young lady ought to visit. I had soon deduced that while it was acceptable to have Madame come along to one's residence for fittings, it was not the thing to go to her. Not that it was crowded or noisy—quite the opposite. She had a tiny sitting room rigged up very stylishly, a waiting room to contain those bodies not actually out back being measured and stuck with pins. In the room sat two dandified gentlemen and a female who was *not* a lady, if you understand my meaning. It was a place to which mistresses were brought by their patrons to be made elegant. My first impulse was to turn on my heel and flee, and how I wish I had done just that! But I did not. I needed a gown of the first stare of fashion, and I needed it very soon.

We were invited to be seated, to await the ministrations of Madame Vigneault. "That is impossible. We are in a great hurry," I said to the clerk. "If Madame is busy, I shall leave."

They were eager enough for our patronage that I was invited behind the silken curtain that set the waiting room off from the shop to speak to Madame at once. "You just have a seat and wait for me, Dorothy. I shan't be a moment," I said. There was a strong inclination to say more; namely, don't speak to that young buck who is ogling you, but as he was less than two yards from me, I could hardly do so. I leveled a cold stare on him that I thought would keep him in his place till my return.

The upshot of it all was that my stare was ineffective. When I came out from behind the silken curtain after my colloquy with Madame some quarter of an hour later, Dorothy was gone. The buck was gone too, not a sign of either of them anywhere. Much as I disliked to speak to the female who drooped over a new issue of *La Belle Assemblée,* I had to do it.

"The young lady? Oh, she left with a gent," the woman said, as calm as you please.

"The gentleman who was with you?" I asked her.

"There's no gent with me. I'm meeting mine here. I didn't notice who she went with, to tell the truth. I went to the smallest room a spell, and when I got back she was just leaving. All I saw was a gent holding the door for her."

"I see. Thank you very much. You wouldn't happen to know the name of that gentleman that was looking at her?"

" 'Fraid I can't help you, Mum," she said in a lackadaisical way, returning to her book.

There is no describing the commotion that was going on inside of me. The only time in my life I was ever so agitated before was once I was minding a neighbor's child for her, and the toddler fell downstairs, becoming unconscious for full three minutes. I thought the child was dead, and I now thought a fate of equal horror had befallen Dorothy. My heart beat tumultuously, there was an eerie ringing in my ears, and a terrible heat in my head, as though the brain was on fire. The worst of it was that it was all my fault. I had brought an innocent young girl under my protection to this haunt of rakes and their mistresses and abandoned her. I was close to insane with worry and guilt and remorse. I began babbling foolishly, trying to discover who the man was, that I might go after him, and rescue Dorothy. The clerk had the names of the two gentlemen who were in the room, but did not know which one I was particularly interested to find, nor did she have any address for either one. "They pay cash," was her unhelpful reply. With panic driving me to the edge of distraction, I dashed out, my plan being to go straight to Lady Synge to tell her what had happened, and let her decide how to recover her daughter, through Bow Street if necessary. It was too serious to allow me to think of protecting my own name. I had done wrong, and must do what I could to rectify the error, even though it meant certain dismissal.

My tilbury dashed through town as though driven by a madwoman. I pushed my nags as never before or since. I actually passed a pair of bucks having a curricle race down Bond Street. They were not going much under fifteen miles an hour either. I pulled up in front of the house and leapt from my seat, flinging the reins behind me. The horses could bolt or run up the stairs behind me, just as they wished. Luckily, the butler sent a boy out to stable them.

I entered the hall gasping, my hat falling from my head, to see Lord Philmot lounging against the door jamb of the saloon with a steely look in his eyes and a frown that would freeze fire. "Where is Lady Synge?" I asked, panting.

"Out. Lucky for you, Miss Fenwick."

"Where is she? I must find her! The worst thing has happened!"

"No, the *worst* thing has been avoided, no thanks to you. I have brought Dottie home. She is abovestairs this minute, sent to her room."

"Oh, thank God!" I sighed, and stumbled past him, trembling from head to toe, to sink on to a sofa. My state of agitation saved me from a blistering scold. His frown changed first to astonishment, then to an expression hovering on concern. Without another word, he poured me a glass of wine and handed it to me. I was shaking so I could not take it from him without spilling a few drops on my skirt. Upon seeing this, he pressed the glass to my lips.

"Have a sip. It will help you. Come now, it is not the end of the world. Dorothy is fine, not nearly so upset as you are yourself."

I heard disjointed, babbling sounds coming from my lips, and was too upset to stop them. "I was so worried when I found her gone. . . . No one knew the man's address. . . . I had no idea . . . Are you sure she's all right?"

He assured me she was, but I still wanted to see for myself. I ran upstairs, just peeped in her door to see she was really there, then I could begin to recover my composure. Oh dear, and begin to face the music! Before returning below, I went to my room to remove my hat and gloves. What a sight greeted me in the mirror! No wonder Philmot had looked surprised. Hair all blown awry, dust powdering my hat and face, and the after effects of shock robbing my cheeks of any color. I looked a perfect nightmare. I repaired such of the ravages as were reparable, then went below to thank Lord Philmot, from the bottom of my heart. Naturally I wished it could have been anyone but he who had rescued Dorothy, but much better he than no one.

He sat, waiting patiently, sipping on a glass of wine, and preparing a lecture that would do justice to my heinous crime without casting me into another spasm of shock. "You are feeling better now?" he asked, with more hope than concern. Oh yes, he was eager to get on with the scold.

63

Hoping to take the wind out of his sails, I entered at once on my apology, liberally laced with gratitude. "Much better, thank you. And thanks to *you*, Lord Philmot. To see Dorothy home safe is all that matters."

"I must disagree. To realize she has taken to such a den as Vigneault's and left quite alone matters a good deal to me. It will undoubtedly not please her mother much either."

"I had no idea what sort of a place Vigneault's was. Lady Synge recommended her to me only yesterday. I dropped off some material to have made up into a gown while Dorothy and I were out driving. I was not away from her much above ten minutes."

"My sister recommended her?" he asked, his brows rising slightly.

"Yes, I asked her for the name of a good modiste, and she recommended Vigneault."

"But why on earth did you go to her, instead of having her come here?" he asked.

"This is not my home, milord. I work here. I meant to do no more than drop the material off. I was never so horrified as when I came out and saw Dottie gone. But how did *you* discover her? Did she tell you why she went off with that man? He must be a friend of the family I expect. She should not have gone off without leaving me a message. That was ill done of her, to frighten me out of my wits for nothing. It shows a lack of consideration I would not have expected in her."

Philmot's stern frown softened to an expression of defense as I spoke. I was not slow in tumbling to what had happened. He had not plucked her from some roué's clutches, as I originally thought. He had entered the shop and carried her off himself. Furthermore, if he had not done it to embarrass and frighten me, it was more than I could believe. It hardly needs mentioning,

I think, that *Dottie's* lack of consideration was strongly emphasized.

"*I* removed her from the shop. She ought not to have been there, and neither should you," he said.

"*You* took her away!" I exclaimed, as though astonished. "I see." I sat a moment wavering, wondering whether my position were strong enough to launch an attack of my own, as I was much inclined to do. He who hesitates is lost. During my indecision, he struck out at me.

"It was imperative to get her out of that place at once. You may imagine how I felt, to enter a room and see my niece, seventeen years of age, chatting to a gazetted fortune hunter and a libertine I would not let into my stables, let alone my drawing room. I acted a little rashly not to leave you word, but the circumstances—so extraordinary!—must be held my excuse. I am sure you agree I did the correct thing."

I did not contradict him with words, but let the scathing glance I bestowed on him deliver some notion of my feelings. "At least no real harm was done. I have learned a good lesson, and will speak to Dorothy about making up to strange gentlemen. Thank you for your—help in this matter. Naturally I shall tell Lady Synge the whole unfortunate tale."

"Do you think that a wise step?" he asked.

"She must be told. I have no wish to hide my error from her. Indeed it would be quite improper." I looked hopefully to see if he had some good refutation for my speech, for of course I was not the least bit eager to tell my employer of the afternoon's escapade.

"It seems a shame to tattle on Dorothy. She will be in deep disgrace. My sister is adamant about such things. It is hardly the child's fault really . . ."

"I don't plan to put the blame on Dorothy! It was *my* error."

"It was Dottie who was making up to Mr. Holmes."

"Her mother must be told. Only think if someone else should tell her, if she should hear it from a friend, she would think me out of reason deceitful."

"None of the persons in that establishment are her friends. She is unlikely to hear it from anyone."

"Madame Vigneault herself might . . . though she would have no way of knowing it was Miss Crowell with me."

"Madame Vigneault is a reasonable woman, exclusive of the prices she charges. She will not mention it," he said, very confidently. "We are all three culpable to some extent: you for taking her there, Dottie for flirting with Holmes, and I for not leaving you a message. Let us keep our errors amongst ourselves. Least said, soonest mended."

"If you really think it is for the best," I answered uncertainly.

"I do. Allow me to pour you another glass of wine. You are still pale. I'm afraid I gave you quite a fright."

"I was horrified," I admitted, holding my glass out for a refill.

"This whole business arose because of a misunderstanding. My sister intends you to treat her house quite as a home. Have the modiste come to you when next you have need of one."

"I shall discuss it with her, certainly. I had not realized the difficulties that would arise in this position I have got myself into."

"It has been inexplicable to me from the start why a young lady who obviously does not have to hire herself should do so," he said, with a face that strongly invited an explanation. I was not about to satisfy his curiosity. The fact was, I *did* need the job, but felt my treatment would be better if that fact remained my own secret.

I proceeded immediately to another subject. "I have

friends, close friends, in town, for instance, who would like to call on me I am sure, but feel they should not. Yes, you are correct, Lord Philmot. I must discuss my situation with your sister."

"These friends you mention—is it Lady Strathacona and her husband?"

"Why yes, my Cousin Deborah and Jack. Do you know them?"

"Very well indeed. Jack is a connection of mine."

"You will be attending their ball then," I said, wondering if there might be a drive there for me. If Lady Synge was not invited, I was in a pickle, for of course I could not drive my tilbury to a ball. This ball loomed as the highlight of the Season for me. I had some hopes it would ease open the door to other similar do's.

"Yes, I shall. Will you attend, Miss Fenwick?"

"I plan to. I expect to be in touch with Deborah about arranging the details of it. She has little experience in such matters. One trembles to think of her trying to decorate a ballroom," I added, with a little laugh.

"Have you decorated many such ballrooms?" he asked, being a touch ironical, I suspected.

"Oh yes. I always worked with her mama, the Marchioness of Monterne, in planning the family balls at Dawlish. The Duchess of Tavistock too considered me her favorite assistant in that line. Of course we shan't have anything so elaborate as the Duchess's last do," I answered in an offhand way.

"How extremely convenient for Lady Strathacona," he said, with a mocking, tight smile at the corner of his lips.

"It is rather. She is a famous tomboy, you must know. I dropped in on her musical party yesterday afternoon, just taking an hour off from Dottie's lessons you know, and poor Deborah had hired herself a very inferior pianist to accompany the Italian soprano that

67

was singing for us. I enjoyed the Scarlatti though." I saw no reason to tell him I had enjoyed it from the hallway, as Debbie would certainly have asked me if she had known I could get away.

"I didn't see you there, Ma'am," he replied, with a quizzing look. I felt a perfect ass, as a blush brightened my face.

"How should you indeed! I did not enter the concert room, but only listened for a moment at the doorway, for I could not take more than a moment off from my work here."

"That would explain why you mistook Haydn for Scarlatti," he said. "Nothing was played but the works of Haydn."

"Is that so? With Dottie chattering my ear off, I did not notice the difference. They are rather similar, don't you think?"

"I have never thought so. You know my sister is not such a tyrant as you believe. She would be happy to have you broaden your own cultural experiences, for the benefit would be sure to rub off on Dottie and Alice eventually."

"A good point. Even your generous sister is not so broad-minded as to excuse me from the schoolroom entirely, and I have been away from Dorothy long enough. Again thank you for your help. I expect I shall see you at the Strathacona's ball, if not before."

"Before then, surely. Do you not attend Debbie's rout party tomorrow evening?"

"No! No, I am too busy," I answered, with a strong feeling of resentment that I had not been invited. I could not but wonder why Debbie had not replied to my notes.

"What a pity. They will be disappointed. So am I. I looked forward to the pleasure of dancing with you. I suppose you will be rooting around Mrs. Ledwell's larder, finding new and expensive items for Synge to purchase. How does the Bodley Range perform?"

This topic was not chosen at random. The Bodley Range had proved unpopular, as Philmot knew very well. Till Cook got on to its whims, she served the meat very poorly cooked. It came either overdone or underdone. Such inconveniences did not pass unmentioned at the Synge table. His lordship never failed to measure a scowl out to me, along with my meat, as he inveighed against the waste of hard-earned money. I cannot imagine it taxed him unduly to place his money in the funds to earn interest, but it sounded better describing it as "hard-earned."

"The Bodley Range continues to be the scourge of the kitchen. I must try to find an evening free to go down and see what Cook is doing wrong."

"She will certainly appreciate that," he answered, and arose to bow himself out, wearing his customary smiling sneer.

Chapter Six

DOTTIE RECEIVED HER SCOLD; I reprimanded myself very severely indeed; Philmot got away before I thought to enquire what he was doing at Vigneault's in the first place (as though I didn't know!), and Lady Synge remained totally in the dark about our misadventure on that afternoon. When my gown arrived, I felt it was worth every guinea and every second of that harrowing afternoon. It was a fairy's outfit, so dainty, so beautifully made, so well fitting. When I hung my mother's little set of diamonds around my neck, I felt ready for anything, even a party at Carlton House with the Prince Regent's set. I was becoming anxious for the receipt of my invitation. I dropped Deborah another note telling her I was very busy, but could spare her a Sunday afternoon if she wished to hear my suggestions regarding decorating her ballroom. I believe she must have gone out of town for a few days, however, for she did not reply. Neither did she come to call. I had consulted with Lady Synge and received delighted permission to have callers, providing they be such stellar callers as my cousin, Lady Strathacona. "I didn't intend inviting the green grocer's wife to visit me," I replied playfully, to let her know I read her meaning, subtly as it was phrased.

The week wore on. We were busy in the schoolroom and around town studying architecture. I decided to give the girls an inkling of the difference between Romanesque, Gothic, Baroque, Renaissance, and so on. I believe I was fairly successful in this venture, for Dottie had not the least difficulty in selecting Westminster Abbey as an outstanding example of Gothic, while Alice discovered and could name the style of a little jewel of early Norman architecture that was quite unknown to me. This was the Chapel of St. John in the White Tower in the Tower of London. Once we spent a rainy afternoon sketching classical columns, adding a pediment or wall behind to complete the balance of the sketch. The girls could now distinguish a Doric from an Ionic from a Corinthian order.

Eager to show off their new knowledge, they took these sketches down to the saloon to show their mama, who was entertaining Lady Roberts again downstairs. Far from being annoyed at an interruption from the schoolroom, Lady Synge was delighted. I was a trifle disconcerted myself to discover Philmot was of the party. I had not seen him since the fracas *chez* Madame Vigneault.

"I was about to send for you," Lady Synge said. "And what has our clever Miss Fenwick been teaching you two girls now? I swear these daughters of mine are going to be bright blue by the time she is finished with them."

"We are learning all about architecture," Alice boasted wildly. "See what we have been doing, Mama. And it is freehand too. No rulers were allowed."

"How nice! Look, Lady Roberts, Alice has done a

drawing of St. George's, in Hanover Square," the proud mother said, passing the sketch along.

"That is not St. George's, Mama," Dorothy corrected at once. "That is an Ionic column you are looking at. St. George's has Corinthian columns."

"Why, there is no difference, my dear. They are all classical columns, but some are fancier than others."

"Oh Mama! Miss Fenwick says only an ignoramus doesn't know the difference. The Corinthian is much more ornate. It has the acanthus leaves on the capital. The top part is called the capital."

Lady Synge smiled proudly at this display of erudition and bad manners on the part of her daughter, but Lord Philmot was frowning heavily. "What has Miss Fenwick to say about a young girl being rude to her mother?" he asked.

"Miss Fenwick was about to demand an apology!" I said, directing a fierce eye at Dottie.

"Why, what is the matter? What have I done?" Dottie demanded. "You said *I* was an ignoramus, Miss Fenwick. You know you did."

She had me over a barrel there, for I had said just that, to awaken her a little to her sublime ignorance. "Do as you're told, Dorothy. Apologize to your mother," I said firmly.

"I'm sorry, Mama, but it *is* shocking that you don't know anything about columns," Dorothy said. She meant no harm really, but the incident brought home Pope's old familiar line, "A little learning is a dangerous thing."

Dottie's blunder robbed the meeting of any charm it might have possessed. Their fairly decent sketches were not enough to cover this horrible lapse into rudeness. Everyone in the room was uncomfortable except Lady Synge, who never seemed to care for anything but showing her friends how clever her Miss

Fenwick was. "Only fancy my girls knowing all about architecture," was her satisfied remark.

"Three columns do not a temple make," Philmot pointed out. "There is more to architecture than that."

"You may be sure she has taught them everything," his sister replied.

"Everything she knows at least," he said, in a deceptively polite tone.

Like myself, his sister ignored him. "They are studying Shakespeare too, Lady Roberts. *Hamlet* they have been reading. 'To be or not to be.' Have I got that right, Miss Fenwick?"

"If you have not, you may rest assured Miss Fenwick will correct you," he told her.

I smiled and told her it was correct, feeling like the worst sort of fool, but not fool enough to be in any doubt as to Philmot's baiting me. Nor was he done with me yet. There was a glint of mischief in his eyes. "What has your analysis of *Hamlet* brought to light?" he enquired.

"Nothing new. It is too well known and studied to be a mystery, but such a standard classic ought to be a part of any educated person's background. His weakness of character, his vacillation, good intentions hampered by lack of fortitude are what we are working on—a sort of character study."

"You would not approve of vacillation, I assume?" he asked.

"One ought always to be ready to do his duty, without hesitation."

"Even when it involves murder?" he pressed on.

"It was the course Shakespeare outlined as the proper one. I feel personally Hamlet might have been satisfied with a lesser revenge. There is a violence I cannot condone in much of Shakespeare, but still his writing is so great that we forgive him his plots. We shall do

73

Coriolanus next, to compare a man of determined action and fortitude with Hamlet."

"His determination did not prevent him from being talked out of destroying Rome by a bunch of women, if memory serves," Philmot pointed out.

"He was not *obstinate*, to be sure. There is nothing admirable in mindless obstinacy."

"I think he was well served to be murdered for his weakness."

"You thought Hamlet should stick at *one* murder, and Coriolanus should sack a whole city! That indicates a strange discrepancy in your thinking, my lord. Perhaps you are not thinking at all, but only arguing."

"She has got you there, Phil," his sister interrupted, with a show of impatience. A *little* revealing of my cleverness was all that was required. I took the hint and hustled the girls back upstairs, to ring a peel over Dottie. But really it *was* shocking that a lady in such a high position should not know a Doric column from a Corinthian.

By the end of the week, we were become bored with architecture, and turned our attention to matters of manners, philosophy and health. We went to Synge's library and retrieved from dim corners such volumes as I considered useful and instructive—some essays by Hannah More, Mrs. Wollstonecraft's *Vindication of the Rights of Women*, the sermons of John Donne, and a book on anatomy. Everything was in a confused jumble in that library, unsorted according to subject matter and untouched by either human hand or a goose wing duster for some months, to judge by the patina of dust the books bore. Dottie, intending no humor I assure you, informed me they *were* carefully sorted, with all the same color books on the same shelf! She was right too. I was not on the lookout for this unexpected trick of aesthetics in a library.

I had in mind a particular book with a gray cover, and with the key to the filing system now in hand, I went to that area. Dr. Ward's *Collected Essays on the Human Species* was there waiting for me. The Duchess of Tavistock had a copy, and had shown it to me once, mentioning it as being unexceptionable. I took it to my own room for perusal later, and found it enormously interesting, full of useful hints to ward off colds and infection. I do not refer to such superstitious rubbish as hanging a garlic about the neck, or placing a roasted onion in the ear, you understand. As long ago as 1797, Dr. Ward was advocating a scientific approach, emphasizing greater cleanliness and a careful control of diet, along with regular exercise. We really must get more exercise. It was the convenience of the tilbury that robbed us of the pleasure of walking.

In the attic we found a dusty old skeleton to transport to the study room. Dottie, so full of life, called it Hector. The servants were frightened to enter the room with Hector hanging there, his bones rattling in the wind and his lower jaw clicking. Before long, we could name all Hector's various parts—over two hundred of them, though of course the ribs and so on made it unnecessary to actually remember two hundred new words. Lady Synge continued enchanted.

"So odd to think of all those bones inside of a body," she said. "Of course, where else would they be?"

"On the *outside* on animals below the vertebrates on the zoological scale," I told her. She laughed gaily, and complimented me on my humor! She supplied many an unintentional laugh herself, though I was careful not to betray my amusement before Dottie.

Our newly discovered book gave us names, pictures and descriptions of the functions of muscles and organs (male, female, and mutual). We went into this subject in great detail, for it proved to fascinate my charges quite as much as it fascinated me. I half wished I might have been a doctor. The heart, liver, lungs—all became familiar to us. Alice, being close to that age where she might soon make a match, took a keen interest in the reproductive organs. It seemed foolishly prudish to act as though these organs held any different quality than the others. God put them in us and on us for man's well-being and for the race's continuance.

There was one drawing showing a foetus growing right inside a human body that caught her attention, for it was a thing that, while known in a sort of vague way, had never been at all clear to either of the girls. Dottie thought that in some undefined manner the baby's head was inside the mother's head, the arms inside her arms, and so on, the whole to be assembled like a carriage just before or after or during labor.

"How uncomfortable it must be, all curled up in a ball for years," she said. "It is a wonder it can ever unwind."

"Not for years, Dottie, for nine months—actually ten lunar months of twenty-eight days each. And of course it is not a whole body at first."

"How is it possible for it to come out, all in one piece? It is too big," she went on.

The diagram was consulted, causing some consternation I must admit to teacher as well as student.

"It's impossible," Dottie declared at last.

"It must be extremely difficult, but it cannot be impossible. We are all here, each of us born in this manner," I assured them. "I'll try to find someone to talk to us about it. Someone who has had a child." Upon consideration, this no longer struck me as a good idea. Such mothers as I had heard discuss the subject vied with one another to make it as gruesome as possible. There was no point in alarming the girls.

The next question was the one I was dreading. "How

did it get in in the first place?" Dottie asked bluntly.

"It grew from a seed," I told her matter-of-factly.

"Where did the seed come from?"

"From the father," I replied, closing up the book rather quickly. I would have told the whole, but was afraid Lady Synge would not approve totally of this aspect of their modern education, for while she professed to be in favor of modernity, she was actually of the old school who spoke of the stork having visited a family. I did not remove the book from the schoolroom. It was there for the girls to examine at their leisure if they wished.

"I know it has something to do with kissing," Dottie told me.

"Yes, as gathering apples has *something* to do with a pie coming out of the oven."

Next day the book was gone. I observed the two sisters to have a peculiar interest in it. It would be seen in one of their rooms, then the other. When finally it got back to my hands, it fell open automatically at that section dealing with reproduction. I think they must, between the two of them, have discovered the awful truth. They did not mention it to me again, nor did I raise the point. We had plenty of other matters to explore.

Chapter Seven

STRANGELY ENOUGH, IT WAS about a different area of learning than the anatomy lesson that I was called on the carpet. I believe it was Philmot who was accountable for it. He called from time to time to take the girls riding in the park on their new mounts he had given them. I was invited to join them, but with no mount and no skill in that field, I politely declined. After having established that I was to be totally in control of Dottie's days, I found it actually a relief to be rid of her for a few hours twice a week, and soothed my conscience with the thought that physical exercise was nearly as important as mental activity. *Mens sana in corpore sano* was a motto I had lettered in Gothic script and kept hung in the classroom. It must have been during one of the rides that Dottie spoke to him of our reading Mary Wollstonecraft.

Such was the man's ignorance that he misconstrued the matter entirely, having apparently learned from one of his literary friends that Mrs. Wollstonecraft had been wed to William Godwin, the dissenting minister turned atheist philosopher of anarchy. Such was his interfering nature that he ran to his sister to report what he had discovered, in lieu of speaking to *me* on the matter. I was a summoned to the saloon. As it happened, I had that day elected to wear an even more modish outfit than usual, and I did not usually dress like a governess. What I had on my back was a pale mauve serge suit, ornamented at the neck with a lace jabot and a cairngorm pin with an amethyst. I planned to take Dottie to a painting exhibition later on, and was dressed for this exalted outing, where one was apt to meet friends. Debbie and Jack, for instance, might very well be there, for while Debbie would have been happy to live in a stable, Jack was somewhat artistic.

"Miss Fenwick, what a smart suit!" was Lady Synge's surprised comment when I entered.

"Thank you." I nodded to acknowledge Philmot's presence, then said, "You wish to see me, Ma'am?"

"To be sure, I do. That is—Philmot thinks . . ." She looked to him for help. I looked the same place, expecting trouble.

"What does Lord Philmot think?" I prompted gently.

At a commanding stare from her brother, she finally spit it out. "It is about your teaching the girls philosophy," she began hesitantly. "That Godwin woman . . ."

"Yes, and what about it?"

"We are not at all sure. . . .That is, Philmot thinks she is not quite the thing, Miss Fenwick."

"Is Lord Philmot familiar with the essay we read?" I asked, with a surprised glance in his direction.

"No, with her history," he shot back, very quickly.

"We are not studying her personal history, Sir, but only her famous essay on education."

"We know what sort of a reputaion she has, without having read the essay," he assured me.

"It comes as news to me if literature can be judged without having read it."

"She was an adulteress, a mother out of wedlock, and when eventually she married, she chose for husband an announced atheist and anarchist. Is *this* what you wish your daughters to be learning?" he demanded, turning from myself to his sister.

"Indeed it is not!" she exclaimed, her cheeks blanching.

"If you are to bar books because of the author's character you might as well forget about literature. Seal up your library shelves. Shakespeare must go, likewise Byron, along with about ninety percent of the Latins and Greeks. You will end up with the sporting magazines and Hannah More," I told her, ignoring her mentor.

"Yes, but—but are you a friend, an acquaintance of Mr. Godwin and his family?" she asked. This, I deduced, was at the bottom of her concern, and not that I had read Mary Wollstonecraft to the girls.

"I have never met the man!"

"You don't approve of his theories?"

"Lady Synge, my father is a Dean! How should I condone atheism? Certainly I am not a follower of Godwin. I think his theories not only foolish but dangerous in the extreme."

"Philmot mentioned as well that Godwin is associated with—free love," she said, to get the whole unpleasant business over with at once.

"Your brother is more familiar with Godwin's theories than I. I do not follow his writings, I confess. What I have heard of them finds no favor with me. You need not fear I am subverting your daughters' ideas. A lady either marries or she remains a respectable spinster. Those are the options open. I recommend no other course. Naturally most young ladies choose matrimony."

"Well, Phil, you have worried me half to death for nothing," she said, turning with a vastly relieved sigh to tap her brother with her fan.

"Just what is it in Mrs. Godwin's essay you feel worth teaching, if not her philosophy?" he enquired, with a look of frustration that I had outwitted him.

"That women have brains, milord, and ought to use them upon occasion. 'I wish to see women reasonable creatures' is the way it is expressed in the essay. Can you disagree with so humble a wish?"

"Not in the least. I have often wished the same thing, but doubt if reading an essay will accomplish it," he answered dampingly.

"*Do* stop being satirical, Philmot," his sister chided. "You know perfectly well Miss Fenwick is not only reasonable, but clever. Very clever indeed."

"Of that there can be no doubt. She was clever enough to secure an excellent position for herself in any case," he replied.

My employer had the sensitivity to blush for her brother's lack of manners, but had not, I regret to relate, the gumption to call him to account. Much as I longed to do it, I could not push incivility so far. I could give it a little nudge, however, and did so, with the greatest pleasure. "I trust she is likewise clever enough to fill that position to her employer's satisfaction. If you have no complaints, Ma'am, I shall return to my duties."

Before she could agree, Philmot spoke up again. I think he had come there for no other reason than to make mischief. "After you have taught them what facts you know, you must try if you can inculcate a few manners into their heads. It was embarrassing to see Dot behave like a hoyden in front of Lady Roberts the other day. I hope you chastised her severely, Miss Fenwick."

"I did."

"As manners form so small a part of your curriculum, may we know what studies you have included in their stead?"

"Besides philosophy, we are presently studying anatomy, health . . ."

"They can name every bone in the body, Phil, and know just what it looks like and is used for," his sister smiled.

"How useful! If they fail to nab a husband due to their poor manners, they can always turn sawbones. But it *is* marriage you train them for, is it not, Ma'am?"

"My aim is to teach them to be reasonable creatures. If their reason leads them to marriage, then they will be ready to assume their duties."

"They will know enough to avoid buying a Bodley Range in any case," he told me, with a mocking smile.

"Of course they will marry!" Lady Synge said angrily.

"If Miss Fenwick succeeds in leading them down the path of sweet reason, I expect they shall. Any *reasonable* woman would, naturally, be married as soon as possible."

This last speech, accompanied as it was by the boldest smirk ever to darken a man's face, was intended as a snipe at my state of single blessedness. Had Lady Synge not been with us, he would have heard a tirade to make his ears sting, but as she was, he could only hear my philosophy in the most polite terms possible. "Marriage does not agree with all women, Sir. As the institution is presently constituted, it places them at a disadvantage. They are placed in a position inferior to their husbands, legally inferior with regard to their rights, properties, and monies."

"They must be protected," he explained, resorting to the oldest lie in law.

"Children and mental defectives must be protected," I objected, "not rational, adult human beings. If a lady does *not* marry, this protection is not considered necessary. Do you think the law is *implying* something, Lord Philmot? To wit, that a lady is weak-minded to have entered into matrimony."

He wanted to laugh; I could see the glint of a smile lurking in his eyes. His pride, however, could not admit to being bested by a woman. "The law implies that in any given match, the husband is likely to be the wiser. The law must operate on probabilities, for there can hardly be a special decree laid down for every case."

"What have you to say to that, Lady Synge? Do you find it the general rule that the husband is of a superior intelligence to his wife?" I asked her with a rallying smile. I had realized for some time now that Synge was a bit of a fool.

"Rubbish! That is what *I* say. I cannot think offhand of a single husband of my acquaintance who is one half so shrewd as his wife. I'll say *this*, Miss Fenwick. They may have the advantage in *law*, but when the doors are closed behind us, we can manage them every time. *I* do just as I wish, and so does every other woman, unless she is a ninnyhammer."

"Take care, Sis. You are calling Miss Fenwick a ninnyhammer," Philmot pointed out.

"Nothing of the sort. She is not married."

"No, she is afraid to marry because she would be legally bound by her husband's wishes. She is too great a ninnyhammer to manage a man, in other words."

"I am not afraid to marry!" I declared.

"That was not what I meant in the least," Lady Synge informed me.

"I simply do not wish to be bothered having to

manage a husband," I explained. "I have better things to do."

"Yes, managing your two brats, Sis," Philmot told his sister. "It seems a waste of so much cleverness on Miss Fenwick's part to spend her talents thus. She should be running Parliament, or a business."

"I should dearly love to give it a try, but my skirts prohibit me from doing so. I could hardly make a worse mess than the cabinet in any case."

"Your talents would have to be broad indeed to make a mess in so many spheres as the cabinet does. It comes to seem it is trousers you ought to be wearing. You could have given the Almighty a bit of advice on which sex you preferred when He was creating you, if only He had given you your tongue before all else."

"Very true, but as He is always considered to be man-like, I daresay He would not have listened."

"No, no! Pray keep your accusations within bounds," he said. "You must admit that when Miss Fenwick speaks, I listen."

"I'm afraid we are shocking your sister by speaking so loosely of our Maker." He was looking so self-satisfied that I began to suspect he had come to draw me out before her, to prove my ineligibility for this job.

I immediately set to repairing the impression I had just made, by mentioning my father's position once again, and reaffirming my belief in the tenets of Christianity. Philmot sat throughout the whole with a sardonic smile on his lips. He knew exactly why I was adding these last remarks. I was extremely annoyed, the more so as I could not do a thing about it in front of my employer. I was ready to crown him when he clapped his hands at the end of my little spiel, and congratulated me on my "speech." I left as soon as I could decently get away, but I did not forget that I had a score to settle with Lord Philmot.

Chapter Eight

MY EX-PUPIL, LADY STRATHACONA, was mentioned daily in the social columns. Two days in a row her ball was written up as one of the great events of the Season. I looked forward to it with no small degree of pleasure, standing each night to admire my new gown before going to bed, and imagining myself in it, whirling under the blazing chandeliers of Strathacona House, with all of polite society around me. The ball, to be held in May, was to have a theme of May Day. I had dozens of ideas to decorate her place, bearing the theme in mind. Even a maypole erected in the middle of the ballroom, trimmed with twining ribbons and flowers, occurred to me as being novel, and possible of managing without interfering with the formal dances in such a large room as her house must have for dancing. A wishing well too would be quaint, and of course buckets of fresh flowers everywhere must be set out. As the date drew ever nearer—a week, then four days, then three, I concluded she had brought in a professional decorator. I did not mind really. It was more consideration than I looked for, for her to realize I was too busy to do it for her. In the past, she was not famous for her consideration.

She was a scatterbrained, inconsiderate girl really, and it was nowhere more evident than in her neglecting to send me a card for her ball. Naturally it was expected I would go. I was practically one of her family after being a full year with them at Dawlish, but would the butler on service at the door know I was expected? The awful image once even popped into my head of being turned from the door because of Debbie's neglect in not sending me a card. Any logistical inconvenience in getting there had been overcome long since. The Synges were going, taking Alice with them, and had invited me to share their carriage. I was grateful for it. It would show Debbie and Jack that I was not by any means a mere governess *chez* Synge. The only detail wanting attention was my invitation. What should I do about it?

It was with great relief that I read next morning of the Marchioness of Monterne's having arrived in town for her daughter's ball. *She* was not so forgetful as Debbie: *she* would not only be sure I had my invitation, but would almost certainly call on me in person, or ask me to Strathacona House to visit her. It was the latter course she followed. Her arrival was enough of an event that I did not hesitate to ask Lady Synge for an hour off in the morning to pay the call. Permission was given most cordially. Certainly I must go and call on my cousin, and must feel perfectly free to invite her to return the call. Lady Synge would be delighted to receive her. There was no surfeit of marchionesses in milady's saloon.

The butler at Debbie's place, who looked about as ugly and self-important as Lord Liverpool, deigned to admit me. He invited me to await her ladyship in a skimpy parlor that I am sure must have been set aside for tradesmen. I no sooner set foot inside the door of the closet than I resented his treatment. "If you will be kind enough to show me to my cousin's ballroom, I shall await her there. Please hurry. I have another appointment," I said in the snippiest voice I own. It is the only kind of treatment for these uppity butlers. He showed me most politely to the ballroom, and nipped off to call Lady Monterne.

The ball was two days away, but already the general configuration of the decorations was visible. Very elaborate indeed. It must have been Jack who consulted with the decorator on the design. He had the same idea as occurred to me—a maypole in the center of the room, and a great deal else besides. The chairs round the room's perimeter were set behind a white picket fence, with here and there a stile to enter the seating area. Potted plants were everywhere, and of course fresh blooms aplenty would be in evidence at a later date. A pale blue silk canopy was attached to conceal the beamed ceiling overhead, with a great sun made of golden paper and puffy clouds fashioned somehow to look very natural. A bucolic atmosphere had been created at some wicked expenditure. I envisaged ladies in panniered gowns like shepherdesses moving amidst the shrubbery. There were even a few stuffed lambs set in amidst the greenery, which probably gave rise to my notion of shepherdesses.

I climbed one of the stiles and took up a position on one of the chairs behind the fence to see whether it were possible for the seated guests to get a good view of the ballroom floor. They would have a flat evening's entertainment if they could not. The neck had to be craned to see around a potted tree, but a pot could always be moved an inch. Glancing at my watch to time my wait, I heard footfalls and voices from a door that stood ajar behind me. It was Debbie, with Lady Monterne, having a squabble about something. They were always at it. I had hoped Debbie's becoming her own mistress might remove them from each other's throat's.

"You certainly *must* ask her. It is inexcusable, Deb, after all she has done for you," the mama was scolding.

"She is such a bossy old scold, Mama. Jack hates her. She has been pestering us . . ."

Before more was said, they spotted me and came forth to greet me, postponing the argument about an unwanted guest at the ball till another time. I knew who they spoke of. There was an Aunt Erma in the family who made it her business to annoy them all. Deb had been warned to call on her, but apparently had not sent her a ticket for the ball. It was so nice to see my cousin again. I pitched myself into the marchioness's arms and received a kiss, as if I were her own daughter. Debbie too was very happy to see me. She apologized profusely about not having returned my notes, but as I suspected all along, she had not realized I was anything but a governess at Synges.

"No, no, I am quite a member of the family," I assured her. "Lady Synge will be delighted to have you both call on me at Russell Square. She told me to be sure to ask you. I am more a guest than anything else at the house. Always dine with the family and their company and have twice gone to the play with them."

"I expect you are also on terms with Lord Philmot then," Debbie said, with a sly smile. I remembered his saying Jack was a connection.

"Yes indeed. We usually have an argument at least once a week, for he is so toplofty there is no bearing it. I never knuckle under to him, but you must not tell his cousin, or Jack will carry tales on me."

"Jack is not his cousin," Debbie told me. "Jack's sister is married to some relation of Philmot's."

"I thought he said he was a cousin."

"No, only a slight connection. Philmot will be happy to hear you have made a mistake, Olivia. He says you are always catching him out in his errors."

"Does he indeed? It comes as news to me. He has never admitted to being in the wrong yet."

"You two have something in common," Debbie said, joking me, for there had been a few items regarding her wedding over which we had disagreed. Jack, for example, had wanted a small wedding, but Lady Monterne wished to make much of the affair, and I tended to agree with her, while Debbie, of course, supported Jack.

"I have nothing at all in common with Philmot. I suppose he comes to your ball?"

"Of course. He and Jack are very good friends. They are together three or four days a week. I like him excessively."

I had not realized they were so close. It was strange Debbie had not asked me to any of her smaller parties when she was so close to my employer's brother. The relationship must have brought me to mind is all I mean, and Philmot could have let her know in short order that I was free to go about socially in the evenings. But there—I would not put it a straw past him to have given her just the opposite idea on purpose to deprive me of pleasure. "He mentioned attending your musical afternoon," I said.

"He told me you dropped by that afternoon, Olivia. Had I known you were here, I would have asked you to stop in and hear Madame Franconi."

"*Signora* Franconi, Debbie," I pointed out. "The lady is Italian, not French. It is a pity you had not known I was here, but there is no harm done. Your butler might have told you I was here. He is very disagreeable, is he not? I would not tolerate his impertinence a moment if he worked for me. You are too soft by half."

"He has worked for Jack's family for several decades," she told me.

"I can only stay a moment," I said. "Your ball is to be one of the great occasions of the Season. I am looking forward to it. I think you have got that picket fence about six inches too high, by the way. Other than that, your decor is very nice. I expect all the ballrooms are done up as gardens this month."

She remembered then that I still had not got my card, and went off to get it for me. Her mama explained away her negligence. "Debbie is so busy, and you know what a sad scatterbrained creature she is, Olivia. Very naughty of her not to have sent it sooner. I gave her a good talking to, you may be sure."

"I think Debbie needs a secretary, Cousin. With her busy schedule it is a wonder she remembers to attend her own parties."

We went to sit in a private parlor, had a good cose about the old times, and a cup of tea. Debbie, so busy with her ball, could not rejoin us. I saw her for a moment again on my way out. Some callers had caught her and were wasting her time, when they must have known how much she would have to do. But Deb would rather gossip and gab than do anything else except ride. I did not see Jack. I expect he was out.

I returned to Russell Square in high gig, my invitation tucked into my reticule, soon to be tucked into the corner of my mirror as a constant reminder of the happy evening awaiting me.

Now at the height of the Season, we saw little of Alice. Her being so often out pitched Dottie and myself into an even closer alliance. The child developed a fondness for me that was quite striking. I often noticed

90

her using my expressions, or physical gestures. Even a little something of my own phrases and tone of voice crept into her talk. She quoted me often to her mother, who never tired of hearing what new tricks she was learning at my expensive elbow.

"Dottie will make an excellent wife for some fortunate gentleman, Synge," she said to her husband one evening over dinner. It was one of the few occasions when there was no company to share the table with us.

He made the humphing sound that passed for conversation with him when he did not wish his eating to be interrupted.

"Salmon again, Mama!" Dottie exclaimed when the fish was set on the table. "It is still scarce and expensive in May. Miss Fenwick says it is more economical to buy the foods that are in season."

"*April*, Dottie," I corrected her. "Salmon is in season in May."

"Oh, it must have been last month you were complaining of our having it three times a week," she said.

Lady Synge smiled and said to her husband, "These two have been making up lists of what foods are in season in each month, to cut down on Cook's costs. I wish Alice could spend more time with Miss Fenwick, but she is become such a rage she is never free."

"Miss Fenwick says there is a shocking amount of waste in the kitchen," Dottie continued. "We saw a mutton shank bone tossed into the garbage with half a pound of meat still on it, that would have made an excellent soup stock. The vegetables too that were hardly wilted a bit were tossed out."

"Seems to me it is *you* ought to be taking lessons from Miss Fenwick," Synge said, with a surly look at his spouse, who passed the look along to me.

"You know you won't touch mutton soup," she told him.

It did not seem the right moment to tell her such leftover meals are for servants. Instead, I upheld her position, for I always had more to do with her than her husband, and it is only common sense to be on terms with one's employer. "In general, there is more money to be saved in the stables than the kitchen, Lord Synge," I said. "Most homes have roughly twice as many horses as they require. Some extravagant men even keep horses stabled at the changing posts along the well-traveled routes."

Lady Synge laughed merrily. "She has got you there, Synge! My husband keeps a team stabled at Reading, Miss Fenwick. I daresay they cost more than the shank bone my cook threw in the garbage."

"*Some* men even stable their governess's horse free of charge," Synge informed me, with an angry eye.

Had I realized Synge had a team at Reading, I would have selected a different example, for there was no point in antagonizing him. To calm him down, I said, "If one practices good economy in other areas, he can well afford to indulge his passion—horses, or whatever. Paying one's debts promptly to avoid interest, not gambling . . ." I was about to continue with more sensible rules of conduct, but it was clear from Synge's glare that he followed none of these rules, so I asked for the hot mustard instead, and ceased speaking of household management altogether. That would be restricted to the schoolroom in future.

Unfortunately, Lady Synge did not follow my lead. It was at about this time she began to pester him about his spending. I don't know if they were short of funds or what, but I know she often gave hints of an economical nature to him, prefacing them with the words, "Miss Fenwick says" more often than I liked.

"When I want a governess's opinion on my bookkeeping, I shall ask her for it!" he exclaimed angrily.

I decided on the spot I would take dinner in my room for a few days, till the air cleared. It was more pleasant than eating with the Synges *en famille,* but when they had company, I would join them.

The night of the Strathacona's ball, they had a good deal of company. Six couples dined with them, including Lord Philmot and his current flirt. Mrs. Dexter, she was called, a widow lady of very dashing appearance and uncertain years, but certainly not on the sunny side of thirty. She had jet black hair and wore a black point de gauze gown with Brussels appliqué that made my mint green, of which I was so proud, look like an outfit for afternoon. She called him "Dahling," and looked as if she would like to eat him.

Chapter Nine

THERE HAD BEEN SOME suggestion at the time of Deb's marriage that I should go to live with her and Jack for a year or so, to put her in the way of holding house. I did not care for the idea in the least, knowing what a third foot I would be in a household of newly-weds. I came to realize at the ball that Debbie stood in need of a few lessons. Her manners had deteriorated into something not much improved from what they were when I first made her acquaintance. Her raucous, hunting voice had reemerged. You could hear her bellow a room away. She was very remiss in her social duties too. I knew no one at the ball except her family and the Synges, yet she did not trouble her head to introduce me to a single, solitary soul, nor even to see that Jack partnered me for a dance. Such were the manners of one of the chief scions of society.

I sat for a full forty-five minutes against the wall with the Marchioness of Monterne and a clutch of dowagers, trying to see over the picket fence that was too high. When the elderly dames arose to make tracks for the card parlor, I determined not to join them, and was sunk to looking about for Alice, a mere child, in hopes of joining her set. There wasn't a gentleman in it older than myself, but one hoped they would have the charity to ask me to stand up. Getting on to the floor was the real problem. Once one got up for one dance, others would observe I was not of the class of spectators, and would, I hoped, ask me to partner them.

The first partner she put forward was Captain Tierney. The name was familiar from occasional references to him made by Dottie. Alice had never breathed a word of her infatuation with the fellow, but it was there to be read in her glowing eyes. Tierney was a well set-up gentleman; any man who is not actually ugly or deformed looks well in a scarlet tunic. He was of medium height, his conversation sensible but not scintillating. His dancing too was passable, without rising to any such level as graceful. I had no real complaint against Tierney. He would do for some genteel lady, but with no fortune or title behind him, I really felt Alice might do better for herself. I knew from Dottie that Lady Synge felt the same.

When Alice shyly asked me, after the dance, what I thought of him, I could not like to praise him too much to her. "He seems gentlemanly," I told her. "There can be no harm in your having a dance with him. I would not stand up for a second if I were you. It would look a little particular, as though you were giving serious consideration to an officer." I gave a light laugh to show her how ineligible any mature person found the idea.

"He is a captain," she pointed out, "not a mere lieutenant."

"Yes, my dear. That is what makes it quite all right for you to have *one* dance with him. Who is the dandified little man you were dancing with just now?"

"That is Harmsworth," she said, with no great enthusiasm.

This name too was more than familiar to me. Alice was often out with him, and he was often in Lady Synge's saloon. He was the suitor favored by her mama, and it was a great pity he should turn out to be what the bucks call "a skirter," which is to say there were some traces of femininity in him. He was small, daintily formed, wearing an outfit that bespoke the dandy. In appearance he did not compare well with Tierney, but how appearances may deceive! When I met him—I asked Alice to present him to me—his superior breeding was clear at once. None of the dull, cloddish trotting out of facts that one heard from a Tierney. No, a peer whose family had been titled for five hundred years, he knew what mode of conversation was eligible for a ball. He was monstrously amusing, very whimsical in his talk.

"Miss Crowell speaks a good deal of you. All she says is to your credit, Ma'am," he began, bowing with a fine flourish.

"Kind of you to say so. I believe I have heard a

mention of yourself as well, milord," I answered, with a civil curtsey.

"Pray do not repeat it! One should speak only well of the dead. I am dead on my feet, you must know. Your charge killed me with a careless word last dance."

"What did the thoughtless girl say to do you in?" I asked, entering into his raillery.

"She said she prefers a scarlet tunic to my puce jacket. Now you must own it was an incredible cruelty. The evening just begun, too. I shall have several hours in which to regret not having worn a scarlet jacket, but I was afraid of being taken for a postman. Lacking only the bell and bag."

"She is not so foolish as she leads you to believe. It is not what jacket a man wears, but what is beneath the cloth that counts."

"I have an unaccountable notion she prefers broad shoulders to narrow as well," he admitted with a charming smile of disparagement.

"Physique is of little account. A plough horse is larger than a thoroughbred, but most folks would prefer the latter I think."

"You are an angel! Will you intercede on my behalf with the fair Alice?"

"When I come to know you better I may, Sir."

"I shall be at pains to know you much better," he said.

So he was, too. One set of dances was not enough for him. He must fetch me a cup of champagne afterwards, and find a secluded corner for us to become better acquainted in. I heard all his family history. He was from Hampshire. "What is called the New Forest area, due to its being one of the oldest forests in the country," he explained. "My ancestors came over with William the Conqueror, as many in the area did. It is believed to have been the hunting that lured my ancestors hither."

Doris, my stepmother, was from the same area, but I made quite sure the descendants of Norman aristocracy were not familiar with her kin, and did not bother to mention the circumstance. "That is where the Red King, William Rufus, was killed in a hunting accident, was it not?"

"Alice told me you know everything. I made sure she was exaggerating, but I see it is not the case. If you say it is where Rufus met his end, let it be so. I daresay one of my ancestors did him in. This dislike of gentlemen who wear red goes back a long way in the family tradition."

"Actually I believe it was his hair that was red."

"Anyone with red hair deserves to be shot. Where are *you* from, Miss Fenwick?"

"My home is in Bath, where my father is Dean, but before coming to London I was staying with my cousins, the Monternes, at Dawlish."

"You are related to Debbie? I had not heard it."

A subtle difference crept into his demeanor at this mention of my family. Not that he was not perfectly respectful before. He was, but respectful in the way of a lord to a lady of uncertain background. He now began treating me as a perfect equal. "Are you also related to Alice?" he asked.

"Only by friendship. I am staying with them till Dottie is out, as a sort of governess," I added, laughing.

"I had come to realize from Alice's frequent references to you that you were an extraordinary lady; I did not half appreciate you till we met. There are not many ladies in your position who would feel it desirable to perform any useful function while awaiting the time they decide to marry. I think it an excellent thing myself. Much more interesting than wilting about a deanery in Bath, and so advantageous for the Crowell girls to have the privilege of your experience for a short space of time."

He understood precisely how my mind worked. "I did find Bath a trifle confining," I admitted. "Particularly after my father remarried. London offers so much. I often have my tilbury harnessed up and take Dottie and Alice to a museum or art exhibit in the afternoon. There are the theaters and routs in the evening."

He nodded approvingly. There was so much admiration in his eyes I was beginning to fear Alice would think I was stealing her beau from her. To remind him of my reason for getting to know him better, I said, "In fact, we plan to visit the new exhibit at Somerset House tomorrow around 2:00. Perhaps we shall see you there? I refer to your asking me to intercede for you with Alice." The last I added in case it sounded as though I were attempting to set up a meeting on my own behalf.

"I shall bear it in mind," he said. He suggested we meet for another dance later on, but I declined, very politely.

I had a place at dinner beside Lady Monterne with a very select party. After dinner, Jack condescended to ask me to stand up for a waltz, and I condescended to accept, as I particularly adore waltzing. He went out of his way to be unpleasant. "I noticed you spending a deal of time with that bleater of a Harmsworth," was his first speech. "Not at all the thing you know, Miss Fenwick."

"A strange way to speak of a guest in your own house, Jack."

"There are plenty of people here I would not care to see a friend or relative become too intimate with. Fortune hunters, rakes . . ."

"Which category do you place Lord Harmsworth in?"

"The former. He ain't man enough to be a dangerous rake."

"He is well spoken of at Synge's house, where he runs quite tame."

"There is a good deal goes on at *that* house that defies rational explanation." I thought there was a dig at their having hired me, but I believe I was looking for offense where none was intended. His next speech was, "You are well needed there, Livvie." I noticed he had slipped from the stiff Miss Fenwick to Livvie, as he used to call me before the wedding. "You might bring some common sense to the household. You can begin by having Synge turn Harmsworth from the door."

I was not of a mind to have an argument at a ball, so complimented him instead on the decor of the ballroom, without mentioning the fence was too high. I asked how he and Debbie were enjoying London. The waltz passed without squabbling and without any invitation to future do's the Strathaconas might be planning. Jack dumped me as quickly as he could, alone at the edge of the floor.

Looking around for a familiar face, I noticed Philmot was regarding me from across the room. He was with a group, mostly female, with Mrs. Dexter protecting her property as best she could. I was piqued he should catch me without a single man to lend me consequence, but only Jack, departing as fast as his two long legs would carry him. Whether Philmot even realized I had been with Jack was debatable. In any case, he was gentleman enough to come to my rescue, and I grateful enough not to be sharp with him, for I was really having a remarkably dull time, after all my high anticipation.

"I was happy to see you steer Harmsworth away from Alice," he said, after the preliminary remarks were finished. "I dislike the way he has been dangling after her lately."

"I was of the opinion your sister approved of him, liked him better than that officer Alice has in her eye."

"Neither one is eligible. Alice is too young to be marrying yet. Another year on the town will do her a world of good. It was kind of you to draw him away a spell, and let her get back in with her own set. Not one of the brighter interludes of your own evening, I fancy."

"On the contrary. I found him amusing and conversable."

"He can be amusing enough when he wants. He must think you are an heiress if he bothered to insinuate himself into favor. It would be the elegance of your toilette led him astray," he added, his glance flickering off my mother's diamonds with a little surprise I think.

"He is pretty well aware of my situation. Is Harmsworth without fortune, or what is amiss with him? His breeding I know to be unexceptionable. His family goes back to the Norman Conquest."

"He's a gambling fool. Been living on tick and postobits for several years. They say he has the bailiff in his house this minute, but that may be an exaggeration. There is money in the family, of course. He may come round one day, if he marries well to tide him over the near term."

"That is not a very uncommon story, is it? Most gentlemen seem to live beyond their means."

"It is because they have not a Miss Fenwick to manage them. Synge has been complaining—ahem, *saying* you have lately taken an interest in his accounts. You'll catch cold at that, Miss Fenwick. Better confine yourself to the girls."

"I do not interfere with Synge in the least. What your sister may have said to him has nothing to do with me."

"That ain't the way *I* hear it. Shall we argue or dance?" he asked, as the sets began forming. "A cotillion. How gay. We must use all our wits to remember the steps and figures, if we are to participate."

"I believe I have wit enough to dance and talk at once."

"I am not so talented. I prefer to argue, if you have no serious objection?"

"If you are not asking me to dance, Philmot, then I cannot very well accept, can I?"

"Extremely logical, as I might have expected from Miss Fenwick, even at a ball. Come, I'll get you half a dozen glasses of champagne, and try if I can make you tipsy to see if you know how to talk foolishly, or are only good for spouting common sense,"

"I hope I am not so ill-bred as to talk sense at a ball!" I answered jokingly, remarking how he, like Harmsworth, displayed that superior breeding that sets the nobleman apart from the rest. I had got enough good blood from my mama that I could keep pace with him. We talked the greatest nonsense for half an hour, during which we consumed two glasses of champagne each, not six.

"I had no idea the redoubtable Miss Fenwick was capable of outright nonsense," he complimented me, before we had conversed for five minutes. He said it in an approving way, with a warm smile. "You ought to drink champagne more often, to loosen your tongue."

"Why, I don't have to be tipsy to talk foolishly, Philmot!"

"We are being nonsensical, not foolish. There is a world of difference. Any dull old fellow might be foolish; nonsense requires a keen mind. It is *intentional* foolishness, and to be lauded as giving the tired brain a rest from rationality."

"A sort of verbal waltz," I went on, expanding on his

thought, "to rest the linguistic legs from the strict pace of the cotillion."

"Precisely. Folks may say what they like about man's differing from the lower animals by his ability to laugh or cry or read French, *I* say it is our talking nonsense that sets us apart. Have you ever heard a dog talk nonsense? Devil a bit of it."

"Of course not! They always want to talk politics or economics."

There was very little sense spoken during the entire half hour. Before he left, Philmot said, "Well it is a great pity you have decided never to marry, Ma'am, for you would be a decided advantage at the head of some gentleman's table."

"Surely he would expect to fill that chair himself."

"Now you are beginning to slip back into sense. I shall take my leave before you compose a lecture on the management of my stables."

Philmot's manners were a cut above Jack's. He presented me to another gentleman and heard him ask me for a dance before he took his departure. The remainder of the evening was excellent, just as I had envisaged. One interesting partner led to another, all gentlemen of the first stare. I think it safe to say I enjoyed myself better than Philmot, whom I happened to spot from time to time. He was not laughing and engaging in nonsense, to judge by his demeanor. In fact, he looked bored, especially when he was with Mrs. Dexter. I went home with my head in a whirl, to be told by my employer I must sleep in late the next morning, as I did at Monternes'.

Chapter Ten

I ENVISAGED A WHOLE new sort of life opening up before me. Now that I had established social contact with Debbie and Jack, I would receive further invitations from them. They had spoken of a water party, for instance, that sounded novel and pleasant. Philmot had been more friendly than formerly. As he was a great friend of Jack, I would see more of him, and by degrees might make the acquaintance of some of his literary friends, such as Miss Burney. While awaiting this prized future, however, a few mishaps occurred.

First, there was the matter of the trip to Somerset House, and the rendezvous with Harmsworth. As it turned out, Alice decided at the last minute not to come with us, which put me into a bit of a quandary. I had said we would be there, and for none of us to show up was too rude. I must go and make our apologies, taking Dottie with me so he saw it was not a ruse on my part to further the acquaintance with him for my own ends. He was desolate, but tried to hide his hurt by being gallant to Dottie and me. He took us on a tour of the portraits, amusing us throughout with very droll stories of the ladies and gentlemen who looked so very proper, but were each and every one a rascal, if half his tales were to be believed. He offered to take us for a drive afterwards, but I had driven in my own tilbury.

"Your own tilbury?" he asked, vastly impressed. "What sort of governess is this who wears diamonds to balls, and has set up her own carriage?"

"Oh a very superior sort of governess, to be sure," I answered.

"Also a very charming one. I hope she is sympathetic as well, and brings Alice to meet me on another occasion."

"Something might be arranged. But you are hardly *persona non grata* at Russell Square, Sir."

"Oh Russell Square," he scoffed. "To be one of her court—that is no good. It is much more romantic to meet her by secret tryst, especially if she is escorted by her governess, to play propriety. Where will you be tomorrow, Ma'am?"

"I fear Alice will not be with us tomorrow."

"Then I shall meet you and Dottie, to make her jealous," he answered quickly.

There was a little touch of seriousness I could not like to encourage. We took our leave, with no promise of meeting him again by appointment.

It was not at all late when we left. Dottie had been plaguing me to give her a few lessons with the ribbons. With this end in view, we drove out of town, towards the Chelsea Road. We turned off down a lane that was completely private, for I did not wish her to encounter any wild bucks hunting the squirrel on her first lesson. She went on famously for a mile, pleased with herself, though it was hardly a challenging trip, a straight road with no other traffic. We were getting rather deep into the country by this time, so I decided to have her turn around. At the first farm, we would do so. Unfortunately, the first farm did not appear. For half a mile we drove onwards, till at last we decided to try to execute a turn in the middle of the road, a thing I would never do in traffic, but with all the time in the world to maneuver, I could see no danger in it. The more fool I!

The thing proved not only difficult; it was impossible. We got the team to turn well enough, though it was necessary for me to take over the ribbons to accomplish it. Once the team were turned, it became obvious the roadway was not wide enough to let the carriage follow without going into the ditch. It proved equally impossible for the carriage to back up to allow the team to resume their normal position in front of it. We were firmly stuck, with the team becoming restive at the edge of the ditch, while the carriage was sideways, blocking the road. No amount of pushing, shoving or urging altered the case an iota. After a quarter of an hour, I decided to try if the carriage could take the ditch and come out with all its wheels intact. To make short work of my story, it could not. Its descent into the ditch, quite a steep one, was more precipitous than I had envisaged. Once it got started, it rushed forward wildly, causing considerable fear for the team, who were pulled sideways behind it. I expect I should have unharnessed them. I did so then, too late.

While Dottie held the reins, I clambered down to investigate what had caused the horrid cracking noises, when my tilbury finally stopped rolling. The wheels were perfectly intact. It was the carriage itself that had broken, snapped in half like a straw, to form a v, the front and rear sticking up into the air, while the center sagged. I was broken-hearted, though I tried not to let Dottie see it.

"How are we to get home, Miss Fenwick?" was her major worry. I was more concerned for the bruise on her left cheekbone. I could not like to take her home damaged, but she was not complaining of any pain at all. The rear end of the carriage had bumped her as it sped into the ditch.

My worries soon turned to my dear tilbury. I was never so fond of any material thing in my life as I had become of it. Replacing it was well nigh impossible, for it had cost me dear. Yet I was loath to do without it. Getting home was the first item of priority, and to this end we looked about for the closest sign of life. There was a cottage in the distance, far away, a good mile across the meadow. We gathered up our skirts, I took the reins of my team, and we were off. We tramped for an age through the long wet grass, doing irreparable harm to our shoes and the hems of our gowns, for they would slip down from time to time. I will say that Dottie was a regular soldier, not whining or carrying on in the least as some girls would have done. Her cheerfulness was not easy to bear, but tears and vaporings would have been infinitely worse.

"We must make the best of a bad situation, as you always say, Miss Fenwick," she reminded me.

The cottager had no carriage to loan us, but only a dog cart. It was impossible to go into town in such a low vehicle, especially when I had Dottie's dignity as well as my own to consider. The solution was for the son of the house to take a message to Russell Square for Lady Synge to send a carriage after us, while the closest coaching house haul away my tilbury. The cottager's wife was very polite, serving us tea while we waited.

I half feared it would be Philmot who came to fetch us, but it was Lord Synge who made the trip. He was highly displeased with the whole venture, asking a dozen times if Dottie had not been hurt, while he probed the bruise on her cheek with his fingers. He took positive delight in telling me the tilbury was ready for the scrap heap, and my team likely suffering from sprains as well. They were not, though one of them had got a cut on the foreleg that required a fomentation. Synge arranged all this for me. He had the foresight to bring a groom with him, who stayed behind to do the necessary.

I was in disgrace at Russell Square. "So unlike you to have an accident, Miss Fenwick!" milady declared, amazed at this everyday occurrence.

"To err is human, Ma'am," I reminded her.

She was not divine enough to forgive without remarking on the ruination of Dottie's good green suit and kid slippers, to say nothing of her eye, that would very likely turn black from a bruise on the cheekbone.

"I shall be happy to purchase new clothing for her, as it was my error," I offered quickly, not without a thought to my blue slippers eaten by Toddles, and never replaced by the family. I made it a point to pay for the clothes, and her mama accepted the money too, the skint.

The next afternoon Philmot dropped around to gloat over the affair. "That's a bad looking bruise," he said, looking for any trace of a mark on Dottie's cheek. We had been fairly successful in concealing it with rice powder. He came to us in the parlor used for lessons on that occasion. "Sore?" he asked her, touching what he imagined to be the bruise.

"Not on that side," I had the pleasure of telling him. "The near-fatal bruise is on her left cheek."

"*You* escaped unharmed?" he asked me. I assured him I was unmaimed.

"I went to have a look at your carriage," was his next surprising statement.

"Synge tells me it is beyond redemption."

"I'm afraid so. You might get a few pounds salvage for the wheels and seat. I happen to know of a good replacement going at a bargain, if you are interested. I shouldn't think you would want to be long without your carriage."

"A tilbury?" I asked, knowing anything more to be utterly beyond me.

"Yes. A friend of mine, Lady Beaton, has set up a high perch phaeton, and wishes to sell her tilbury."

"What price is she asking for it?"

"A hundred guineas. I shall speak to her, if you are interested. It will be snapped up in short order."

I wanted the carriage, but was not at all sure I could afford it. Between outfits and the incidental expenses involved in going to museums and so on, I was running short. If I bought the tilbury, I would be at about the bottom of my purse. Yet to be without one would curb my style sharply.

He was regarding me in a questioning way. "Is it out of the question, financially?" he asked frankly.

I was not about to admit I was so purse-pinched. "No. I am interested. Of course I should have to see it before making up my mind."

"I did not expect *you,* of all people, to buy a pig in a poke, I have a better opinion of you than that. We can go to see it now if you wish." He glanced to Dottie, who arose, ready for the outing.

"I'll ask Mama if we may go," she said, and sprinted out.

"With luck, we may get away without her," he said, wearing a peculiar expression. There was a smile in it, along with some tinge of embarrassment. Perhaps the latter was due to the way my lips fell open at the suggestion we were to go alone. In my astonishment, I said nothing for longer than was seemly. It was Philmot who broke the silence. "I was hoping we might have another chance to speak nonsense, as we did at the ball. It was the most enjoyable part of the evening, in my estimation. I shan't put you on the spot by asking

108

for any comparisons. Harmsworth I know found favor with his own brand of idiocy, which leads me to hope you are not overly demanding in your conversational partners."

"I found the whole evening pleasant in the extreme," I told him, refusing to be drawn out into any more of this talk that bordered on flirtation.

"You must promise to reserve me another half hour when you come to my ball. I shall be sending out the cards soon."

I was gratified beyond words. "Thank you. I look forward to it," was the only reply I could think of.

Dottie came pouncing back in, with her bonnet already on her head. I thought Philmot looked a little disappointed. I know I felt inordinately so.

Lady Beaton lived on Upper Grosvenor Square, just at the fringe area of the town. I did not meet her at all. It happened she was out, but Philmot was well enough known to her that he took us around to the stable to view the tilbury. It was not dissimilar to my own, but was green rather than blue, with very ornate gilt panels down the sides. I thought it a bargain at the price, and agreed to take it on the spot. Philmot handled the whole transaction—took my cheque and promised he would see the rig delivered to Synge's stables for me.

"She must be a good friend of yours, to let you handle her transactions for her," I mentioned as we sped homewards.

"She is a connection of my family," he answered, and said no more. I was curious to see the lady, the more so when I took the idea he did not wish to discuss her.

Lord Synge was happy to remind me, every time I called the tilbury, to drive carefully. I feared he might forbid Dottie to drive with me, but it did not come to that. Once I had paid for it, a host of small bills came showering down on me. There was the matter of books ordered that I had given up on ever receiving, there was a modiste's bill for a suit for Dottie. I had thought purchasing the material sufficient recompense for a muddied hem, but Lady Synge meant to exact the full toll. Enough other similar items requiring cash descended on me that I was soon at the very bottom of my purse. If I wished to continue any semblance of fashionable life, I must sell something. Gloves tore to shreds in a few weeks with handling the ribbons, shoes scuffed beyond repair while trekking through the meadow, hats seen too often and such things had to be replaced somehow. I had a few trinkets I did not mind parting with, but was reluctant to go in person to lay them on the shelf. At the very least, privacy was required to do it.

One afternoon when Lady Synge was free, I asked permission to call on Lady Monterne, planning to make a quick trip to a pawn shop en route, though I would certainly call on my cousin as well. Her not having called on me led me to fear she was ill. "It is certainly odd she has not been to call," Lady Synge said. "Certainly you may go, Miss Fenwick, but don't be late."

She would not have added that reminder before the accident. I had slipped a notch in her estimation to have landed my rig in a ditch. As she had said it, I omitted to call on Lady Monterne altogether and went directly to a pawn shop. I selected one I had passed a few times on Tottenham Court Road as being the closest one a female would dare to enter. It was a dismal place. The very dregs of society were there—fops and dandies bartering their watches for a guinea, actresses peddling paste necklaces, and pickpockets keeping a sharp eye on the door. In I went, feeling as out of place as a rose in a turnip patch, to stand in line with these rejects from the polite world. I kept a tight grasp on my reticule and my back to the door, lest anyone passing by should recognize me. The proprietor eventually took my nice garnet brooch and emerald ring in his dirty fingers, shook them a moment, and quoted me a price of a pound. A single pound mind you, twenty shillings, for genuine family heirlooms. He did not know the difference between precious stones and glass. When I pointed out to him that emerald in my ring was close to a carat, he hunched his shoulders.

"A pound. Take it or leave it."

"I shall leave it. Thank you very much," I replied icily, and held out my hand for my jewelry.

"Make it a guinea," he offered. I did not deign to reply to this insult, but walked briskly to the door.

Had I stopped to consider it, I suppose the person I would have liked least to see me in such a place after Philmot must have been Lord Harmsworth. It will come as no surprise to you then that I met one of these gentlemen coming in as I walked out. It was Harmsworth. I was ready to blush at being discovered in such a predicament, till it struck me he was in as tight a strait as I was myself, without showing anything but delight at having met me.

"You have come a cropper too, Miss Fenwick," he said, making light of it. So well bred. He did not wish to cause me any embarrassment.

"I have had a run of bad luck," I told him. I told him in a quiet aside as well that he would be fleeced if he meant to leave his watch here.

"There is no such thing as a *good* bargain when you are in the suds, Ma'am. They are all alike. What is it you are pawning?"

My unhappy glances towards the proprietor let him know I did not wish to talk here. We went outside, where I showed him my baubles.

"Pretty little trinkets, but you will not get more than

a guinea for them anywhere in the city," he told me.

I explained about my wrecked tilbury, and the matter of my being short of cash till quarter day, still some time hence. "What you must do is hawk those diamonds you had on the other night," he advised me.

"I could never do that. They belonged to my mother —family heirlooms."

"I know a fellow will hold them for you till quarter day. He is reliable. Unfortunately, it is not the sort of a place a lady can well enter."

"How much do you think I would get for them? You have seen the necklace."

"Perhaps fifty guineas," he said consideringly.

"Only fifty? Surely they should bring a hundred at least!"

"They are worth more of course, but as you will be redeeming them, you see, it is only a loan with your diamonds standing as collateral."

"Yes, that's true," I said. Certainly I meant to redeem them when I got my next quarter's salary. This was the expensive season. Once summer came, my expenditures would sink sharply, but for the present I did wish to keep up a good appearance, and continue socializing.

"Let me do it for you, Miss Fenwick. I will be happy to help you out of this tight corner. We paupers must stick together." He laughed as he spoke. Lord Harmsworth certainly did not *look* like a pauper, and Philmot himself had said there was money in the family. "I shall be dropping by Russell Square tomorrow morning," he went on. "Slip them to me then, and I'll return you your money the next day."

I hastily considered this solution. A lord who came calling socially on my employer was not the sort of person whose character one could mistrust. I was happy too that he was not the toplofty sort who exhorted me to live within my means and be thrifty, as my papa was wont to do. Mama, on the other hand, who was connected with the aristocracy, had a much freer attitude towards money. A sort of noble contempt for it, like Harmsworth.

"Very well. You are very kind, Lord Harmsworth. I'll slip you the necklace tomorrow, and await my fifty guineas. Meanwhile, the world will be deprived of a sight of my diamonds. I must sink to pearls till I retrieve them."

"You'll not be the only lady in such a pucker," he said, smiling. "Now I shall go in and lay my watch down. It thinks it lives there. Spends half its life on one pawn shop shelf or another."

He left, and I returned to my tilbury, insensibly pleased with my outing. It was well to have a few friends from the ton, to lend one a hand in life's difficulties. What with Lord Philmot procuring me a carriage at a good price and Lord Harmsworth taking care of my diamonds, I was becoming quite a grand lady. The business took such a short while I decided to drop in on Lady Monterne after all. It was well I did, for I made a shocking discovery. She was on the point of departure, to return home to Dawlish.

"I'm so glad you dropped by, Livvie," she said. "I had hoped to get over to see you before leaving, but in the end had to write a note instead. Here it is, you might as well take it. It has a bit of news of the family from home. Deb and Jack are so busy I cannot keep up the pace. They haven't left me a moment free to go and see you. I will be happier back in the country."

"Where are Deb and Jack?" I asked, thinking a sight of me might remind them I was occasionally free to join in their frolics.

"They are having their water party this afternoon. It is what finally made me decide to leave. I detest water parties, with the sun and flies and people splashing and making a great racket. Just the sort of do you would hate, for we always felt exactly the same about such things. And Livvie, my dear, if things don't work out at Synges . . ."

She stopped and cast a commiserating glance at me. "Why should they not work out? I am very happy, doing useful work and enjoying myself into the bargain."

"Yes, but if things become less pleasant, you know I will always welcome you at Dawlish. Sylvia is becoming a rare handful. I could use you very well. And now I really must be off. Write me a line once in a while."

I left with my head in a spin. Why had she intimated I would be unhappy at Synges? I suspected the fine hand of Jack in this affair. He had never cared a great deal for me. I was beginning to think he had exerted some influence over Debbie to exclude me from their parties. This was bad enough, but as he was a friend of Philmot, I was concerned what he might have said in that quarter. From Philmot it would not be long passing to Lady Synge. A sense of resentment, once born, has a way of spreading. Soon I found myself resenting that Lady Monterne had never once called; that she was leaving without so much as telling me beforehand. Even her offer to go to Dawlish had a slight in it. She could *use* me. If she cared to *use* me again, she would find the price had risen from zero to four hundred guineas per annum.

When I returned to Russell Square, Lady Synge asked me how my relatives were. I told her I had seen Lady Monterne. "She is leaving today, which is why I particularly wished to see her."

"How did you know?" she asked, with an astute look on her face. "She has never once been to call on you. How did you know she was leaving today?"

114

I had her letter in my hand. "She dropped me a note and asked me to go to her, as she was too busy to come to me," I answered.

The wretched woman reached out her hand and took the note, to look at the seal to ascertain it was indeed from Lady Monterne. She hadn't even the common decency to look ashamed when she saw it was.

"She most particularly begged me to return to Dawlish with her, but of course I told her I was committed to you for a year," I said.

"Dottie is waiting for you abovestairs," was her answer. "Perhaps you ought to stay in today and teach her something. I cannot believe racketing around the streets and having accidents is the way to instruct a young lady."

"Clever Miss Fenwick" had taken a deep plunge in prestige. "Have you any suggestions, Ma'am?" I asked boldly. "About the curriculum I mean."

"How the deuce should I know? It is your job. I am paying you enough to do it," she retaliated, and flung into her saloon before I could give her an answer.

When I entered the schoolroom, Dottie was sitting at her desk in a perfectly ladylike posture, reading Voltaire, in French. My heart lifted to see how much progress she had made since my coming. I well remembered her sprawl on that day, and her sister's reading matter. I saw the improvement, even if her own mama did not.

"Bonjour, Mademoiselle," I said, to encourage her use of French. After a few exchanges in that language, we reverted to English. "What is new?" I asked her.

"Nothing. Uncle Phil was here, in a wretched mood."

I suspected at once his visit had to do with carrying tales about myself, which would account for his sister's attack of venom. "What caused his mood?" I asked.

"His secretary has left him, and he had to write his own letters."

115

"Is that all?"

"That is enough to put *him* in a pelter. His temperament is rather unstable, don't you think, Miss Fenwick?" she asked.

Though I agreed, I felt compelled to mention it was not for youngsters to judge their elders. "Maybe I ought not to have mentioned it, but I know you won't mind my *thinking* and *judging* for myself, for you have often said people should do so," she pointed out.

"Very true, but be sure you do not say such things in front of your mama. Or uncle," I added carefully.

"I mean to keep out of Mama's way this week. She is angry with Alice, and takes it out on me, only because I am here."

"Why is she angry with Alice?"

"Harmsworth wants to marry her, and Mama wants it too, but Alice wants to marry Captain Tierney, and Uncle Phil doesn't want her to marry anyone."

"Poor Alice. And what does her papa want?"

"He wants them all to leave the poor girl alone he says, but he means he doesn't want to hear all the squabbling. Who do *you* think she should marry, Miss Fenwick?"

"If the choice were mine, I should choose Harmsworth, but if she actively dislikes him, I do not think she ought to marry either one."

"She does not hate Harmsworth so much as love Captain Tierney. Will you marry for love?"

"If I ever marry, it will be a man I can love, certainly, but I shall take some care not to go falling in love with an officer. It would be a nomad's life, following the drum in foreign countries."

"What is a nomad?" she asked. I was happy to divert the topic, happier still to see her taking such a keen interest in increasing her vocabulary, in keeping her ears open to learn new facts.

For the immediate present, it seemed a good idea to practice caution till Lady Synge got over her fit of pique. Dottie and I remained at home that afternoon and got down to some good hard lessons. I hoped to find a moment to speak to Alice, but she did not join us at all. I believe she knew my feelings about her captain, and avoided me on purpose.

Chapter Eleven

I WAS AT PAINS to be on hand when Harmsworth came to call on Miss Crowell the next day. This was accomplished by watching for his arrival from the window in Dottie's room, where we chose to study on that occasion. I slid swiftly downstairs and passed my parcel to him before he entered the saloon. He accepted it with a silent wink. Just what procedure would be employed to transfer the money back to me was not set upon, but I supposed he would return the next morning, and trusted his ingenuity.

Meanwhile, there was a day to be got in somehow. It turned out to be a fine day, and a perfectly wretched evening. But first for the day. Some cousins of Lady

Synge had landed in town for a piece of the Season, and were putting up with relatives in Berkeley Square. They had, apparently, a daughter whom they optimistically hoped to see shot off in a few weeks. The papa was a bishop. As there was a daughter in the party, Dottie and Alice were taken along, leaving me free. I cherished these days of freedom. It was a great pity Lady Monterne had left the city, for it would have been an excellent occasion to visit her.

I have not thus far mentioned them, but my father also had some relations in the city whom I had not yet gotten around to calling on. They lived rather away from the center of things, out in Hans Town. The paterfamilias was a retired sea captain. They did not live in a high way, but the house was genteel and the family had been educated. Piano, books, carpeted stairway and other marks of gentility were in evidence. The wife was lively, a gossipy soul who reveled in my tales of the ton. As it gave her so much pleasure to hear the words "Marchioness," "Lord" and "Lady," I sprinkled them liberally over my talk.

"Your mama's sister married some cousin of the Monternes, did she not?" Captain Danner asked.

"My mama was part of the family herself," I informed him.

"Ah, that would be why you're so interested in all these aristo people. Not much use for them myself. They put on their trousers one leg at a time like the rest of us, when all's said and done."

"True," his wife told him with a sage nod, "but the trousers have deeper pocket, eh Olivia?"

"I hope you have not taken the absurd idea I am impressed with a title, only because the people I associate with are all lords and ladies. You may be sure they will be saying there is nothing but a sea captain for me, when I go back to Russell Square talking of *you*, Captain Danner." I rallied him.

"You could do worse, Dear," Mrs. Danner told me.

I did not mean to stay so long, but somehow the whole afternoon slipped away, and I got back to Synges just in time to change for dinner. Lady Synge was awaiting me in my room. I was astonished to see her making free of my desk and library. "Can I be of help to you, Ma'am?" I asked in my frostiest manner.

Her puffed breast and liverish face told me there was something amiss. "It is a fine thing when I pay you four hundred guineas a year, and you are away all day long," she said, her eyes snapping.

"I was told the girls would be occupied all afternoon," I pointed out.

"It is a great pity I ever took them to meet the Fowlers," she said. "Not that I mean to say for a second it is *Dottie's* fault." The accusing eye told me that whatever had occurred, the blame lay in my dish and no other.

"Suppose you tell me what I have done, so that I can make some sense of this conversation," I suggested. I set aside my bonnet, removed my pelisse and shook it out before hanging it up, to show her how little I was moved by all her agitation and angry looks.

"What happened, Miss Fenwick," she said, drawing in her breath till I feared she would burst her corset, "is that Dottie took the ill-conceived notion of relating to Miss Fowler the *lascivious* stories you have been feeding her about . . ." She stopped and braced herself for the horrendous word. It came out in a gasp. *"Sex!"*

Though I was ready to wring Dottie's little white neck, I answered offhandedly. "Why Ma'am, you do me too much credit to infer I invited the whole. I did not feed her any stories, but the truth. I feared it was something serious, when you forgot yourself to the

119

extent of coming into my room when I was not here."

"It is extremely serious indeed when a bishop and his wife tell me to my face my daughter is a trollop, and they do not wish Dolores to meet with her in future."

"I should not think you would wish to meet again with such insular people," I replied, sinking to the side of the bed in shock and regret, both carefully concealed, it goes without saying.

"Insular indeed!" she bristled, and would no doubt have said more had she had the least idea what the word meant. "You said you had nothing to do with that unholy Godwin person," was her next shot, which was at last a charge of which I was innocent. "The Bishop says he is an atheist!"

"I believe it is so, but I have never met the man. You knew perfectly well I was teaching the girls about the body and its functions," I went on, pressing my advantage, and my luck.

"Bones and veins and muscles, Miss Fenwick! Not all that other wretched stuff."

"I must say it is a fine thing when a *bishop* sets himself up to criticize the works of the Almighty," I said, gaining courage at her muddling way of taking me to task. "One wonders who is the atheist, he or Mr. Godwin. If God in his wisdom has devised the way in which he wishes the human race to be continued, I cannot think it was His intention that we keep it a secret from young ladies. Did you want the girls to gain their theories from kitchen maids and modistes, Lady Synge? I assure you it is not the way it is done in the *better* homes nowadays. Lady Monterne saw to it *her* girls knew all there was to know on the matter before they left the schoolroom. The Duchess of Tavistock as well. In fact, I used the same text as the Duchess. Dr. Ward's excellent book. You are familiar with it no doubt, with your keen interest in modern education. I was happy to see you had a copy on your shelves."

"But Dottie is only a child!"

"She will be out next year. She is physically a woman now. When did you intend telling her the facts of life? The night before her wedding, to send her to do her duties in a state of shock? I cannot believe you to be so foolish."

"Yes, but she told Dolores, and the Fowlers are so old-fashioned there is no bearing it."

"They sound positively Gothic," I answered quickly, wishing her to continue on this track.

"You should have seen the outfit on her!" she told me, happy to get into territory with which she was familiar. "She wore a riding-coat dress with three collars. I haven't seen one since the French Revolution. And Dolores wearing a cap and a gown with long sleeves. I swear the girl had on ten pounds of clothing."

"I expect they told her she was delivered by the stork," I said, risking a laugh.

"It is as much as she'll ever have to know, for if they think to find a match for *that* one they will be disappointed. There is not a *parti* in London would touch her with a pair of tongs. Lady Monterne told the girls the whole of it?" she asked, with a conniving face.

"There was not much they did not know. Debbie was delivering foals when she was twelve."

"And the Duchess as well?"

"But of course. She holds the modern view in education, as all enlightened ladies do now."

I relaxed, knowing a mere bishop hadn't a chance against a marchioness and a duchess. "To be sure we do. Mrs. Fowler is little short of an antique," she confided.

"Of course I had not meant for Dottie to broadcast our medical lectures abroad. I must speak to her about it. She is a trifle indiscreet, don't you think?"

"A hoyden, but she is much better than she was before you came to us, Miss Fenwick."

I had turned her around, saving my skin in the process, or so I thought. Her next remark caused me to suffer a doubt. "Synge feels I should ... but I can always talk him around."

"What does he feel?" I asked, determined to know the whole of my disgrace.

"He mentioned trying to get Miss Silver back . . ."

Miss Silver was my predecessor. Lord Synge thought, in other words, that I should be tossed out on my ear. I weighed in my mind the wisdom of pointing out that I had a contract which I would expect to see honored with cash whether I stayed or not, versus a cavalier and immediate offer to leave them to return to Lady Monterne. I judged the latter to be more likely of impressing my employer. "It is a great pity I had not known it yesterday, and I could have returned to Dawlish with my cousin," I said, in a weary, impatient way that hid all my fears.

"Rubbish!" she exclaimed, pushing herself up from the chair with two hands in a graceless manner. "I can handle Synge. I want my gels to have a good modern education. I shall tell him what you said. Only fancy Bishop Fowler being next door to an atheist," she said, shaking her head as she waddled towards the door.

"He means no harm. Older churchmen always want to stop the clock. Papa has often mentioned it. They would still be stoning sinners in the public square if each new generation did not take some step towards ameliorating conditions."

"Perfectly true," she agreed, nodding her head and storing up the phrase for transmitting to her spouse.

"I have a touch of migraine," was my next speech, to remove the last difficulty from her path. She would bring her husband round her thumb in privacy. "Would you mind terribly if I had dinner in my room?"

"Not in the least, Miss Fenwick," she assured me with genuine feeling. "We'll talk again tomorrow, after I have told Synge how antique the Fowlers are. Imagine Dolores wearing caps, when she was brought here for the purpose of nabbing a fellow." The door opened and I was left alone, to tremble at the closeness of my escape. Indeed the affair had the inexplicable result of reinstating me in the lady's good graces.

An afternoon, especially when a lady has her own carriage, can be got in very agreeably. An evening somewhat less so. In short, I was bored to flinders, sitting alone in my room, for Dottie did not come to me, and I was not so eager to see her minx's face that I went after her. I read, wrote a letter home to Papa and Doris telling them I had been to visit the Danners. It would please Papa. He had asked twice whether I had been to call on them. Next I took the resolution to arise early, which made an excellent excuse to retire early as well. I am not usually in bed with the tapers extinguished by ten o'clock, but I was on that night, when Dottie came tapping at my door, with her nightgown on.

"I'm sorry I disgraced you, Miss Fenwick," she said in a penitential voice.

"You did not disgrace me, my dear. Not in the least, though your mama and I have decided it is better if you not discuss our medical lectures outside of the class-room. In future, we . . . "

"But are you not leaving?" she asked. I could not see her face, but I knew the look it wore—surprise.

"No indeed I am not."

"Papa said . . ."

I lay in trepidation, wondering if Lady Synge had failed to conciliate her husband. I supposed the lord of the house had the final say, if he chose to be stubborn about it. "What did he say?"

"He said he never wanted to hear the name Miss Fenwick again," the artless soul told me.

No sleep was possible after that. I lit the taper, while Dottie curled up on the bed for a chat. She was very sorry, very hopeful, and in the end very unsure of the outcome, but it was perfectly clear to me that I was as welcome as a bailiff in the house. Dottie started sniffling, saying it was all her fault. She worked herself into a substantial lather. When I finally got her into her own bed, she had the migraine and a spot of fever, but I thought it was her mood that accounted for it.

My own was worse. On top of regret, I had some very real fears for my future. Without my continued salary, I could not redeem Mama's diamonds. I could hardly go home without them. I had a welcome at Monternes' in the country, but I felt the offer little better than an insult, coached in such terms as it was. I would have accepted an invitation to go to Debbie and Jack, but knew the chances of receiving one were so slim as to be negligible. One thing I knew, I would not stay where I was if his lordship planned to relegate me solely to the schoolroom. I had come as a guest-governess; I had no notion of relinquishing the more enjoyable part of my status. I had the consolation at least of fifty guineas coming to me from Harmsworth in the morning. That would see me home, to Monternes', or put up at an hotel while I looked for another spot. There must be another modern-minded mother in the city who would hire me.

Chapter Twelve

THE NEXT DAY BROUGHT fresh problems. In the view of the family, the more serious was that Dottie had come down with a raging fever. The doctor was called and diagnosed an extremely virulent dose of chicken pox. I had managed to escape that childish malady, and had not the least desire to contract it at my age. If I had not already become infected after such close contact with Dottie, it would be a wonder. Lady Synge, not having achieved total success in turning Synge to her way of thinking, used it as an excuse to be rid of me temporarily.

"How fortunate your cousins, the Strathaconas, are in the city. You must go to them for a few weeks, Miss Fenwick," she advised me.

I opened my lips to object, but she continued talking. "While you are away, I shall bring Synge to see reason. A couple of weeks should accomplish it. Sit right down and send Lady Strathacona off a note telling her you are coming. You can use my carriage to have your trunks removed. You would not want to ruin the springs of your light rig."

"I am not at all sure they will be staying in town," I told her.

"All the better. Go with them wherever they are going, for there will be a little talk about yourself. Mrs. Fowler is a wicked gossip. She is a positive antique, but she will be meeting many of the ton. It will be a nine days wonder. After Dottie is better and the Fowlers have left the city, you can come back to us and resume your work. I daresay you will enjoy the rest. Naturally I shall continue paying your salary."

The matter of money loomed as large in my mind as being kicked out. I had to remain in the house till Harmsworth brought me mine, along with the important ticket that would allow me to redeem my necklace when I received my next allowance. Writing to Deb formed an excuse to linger till he came. Of course I did not actually write the letter Lady Synge suggested. With her servant waiting, I had to send something, but it was a perfectly pointless epistle, telling her of Dottie's illness, and that I would not be able to see her for a while. If she *asked* me to join her, that was something else. In the worst case, I was toying with the idea of taking to my bed and pretending I had caught the disease from Dottie. The lack of spots was all that stayed my hand.

There was one saving shred to my self-esteem in the affair. Deb condescended to return an answer in which she told me a secret not yet known to society. She was increasing. With such an excellent excuse not to have to invite me to her (disease in the house), she expressed every regret that she could not do so. This unexceptionable reply was shown to Lady Synge, who clucked and said perhaps it was better for me to go to Lady Monterne after all.

While we were still talking, her brother was shown in. "Phil, the worst thing imaginable," she said, then went on to empty her budget to him.

"What exactly is the nature of Miss Fenwick's transgression?" he enquired, upon hearing that Synge was in a bad skin.

"There was no transgression in the least," she told him, to my infinite relief. "That old dowd of a Mrs. Fowler took offence that Dottie did not think she had been delivered by the stork."

"I trust Miss Fenwick has informed both your daughters they were found under a cabbage leaf?" he asked blandly.

"He is jesting," she told me. "Philmot always wastes precious time in joking when there is serious work to be done. Naturally she told them the truth, as all modern mothers are doing nowadays," she said, turning her head to him.

"What an old-fashioned bunch of friends I must have!"

"I expect they are only more discreet than Dottie. Naturally we have told her she is not to repeat the story," Lady Synge told him for me. She had learned all her answers very well.

"What will you do till Synge comes down out of the trees?" he asked me, with no great display of interest.

"It is the chicken pox that causes her to leave," Lady Synge insisted. "She will have to go to Monternes' or home." She looked to me for a decision.

"You prefer work to leisure, if I recall your preference aright," he said.

"Yes. I wish there were someone else in the city who needed a governess for a few weeks. It would save a great deal of pointless travel."

"Is that all you can do—be a governess?" he asked, with a certain pointedness that I could not understand.

"I am not a nursemaid, nor a modiste," I answered pretty sharply.

"You once expressed an interest in running for Parliament, or getting into business, did you not?"

"Oh really Philmot," his sister said, exasperated. "What nonsense are you talking now? Miss Fenwick cannot run for Parliament."

"Have you a seat you are trying to find someone for?" I enquired, wondering how I might fit into his scheme.

"No, not a seat in Parliament, only an empty desk in my study. My secretary has left me. I told you so the other day, Sis. Would you care to give the job a try, Miss Fenwick?"

"If you have nothing sensible to say, pray leave and let us discuss it alone," his sister begged. She was quite distraught.

"That is impossible," I said. "What would people say?" My first jolt of shock had soon subsided, allowing the advantages of the scheme to emerge. Philmot's early disapproval of me had slowly lessened, till at last his behavior was bordering on the gallant. He had claimed to have enjoyed my company at the ball, and indicated a wish to have more of it on the day he got Lady Beaton's carriage for me. I am not a wide-eyed optimist, but stranger things have happened than a Dean's daughter marrying an earl. There, it is out in the open. I had not quite set my cap for him, but if he gave any indication of dangling after me, I was not about to depress him.

"Who would know?" he asked. Lady Synge wore her conniving face. He spoke on calmly. "There is contagion in the house. The governess needs somewhere to spend a few weeks. I am your employer's brother. My home, though a bachelor's establishment, is chaperoned by an elderly female aunt. What you do there is no one's business but our own."

128

I looked to Lady Synge. Lady Synge looked to me. We both wished to say yes, and felt we should say no. "Of course if you feel the work is beyond your capabilities . . ." Philmot said, casting a challenging look in my direction.

"What would the work consist of?" I asked, damping down my interest till the sister should press me a little to take the job.

"Doing my correspondence for me. I require someone capable enough that I can give my decision on matters and he—or she—compose the reply herself. It saves a great deal of time. There are many government reports I have not time to read in full. My secretary reads them and briefs me. Some help in researching speeches I make in Parliament, a little bookkeeping if you have a head for figures. My last secretary, Harding, did all that, but of course when one is making do with a temporary replacement, any help that can be given is appreciated. I would reimburse you for that portion of Miss Fenwick's time I borrowed." He added aside to his sister.

It was too good an offer for her to refuse. "It sounds very interesting to be sure," she told me.

"I don't know about those reports from the government," I cautioned him. Writing letters when the material necessary had been told me presented no problems, neither did I feel incapable of a spot of account keeping.

"Why Miss Fenwick, you are always talking politics," Lady Synge said. "She knows more about politics than most men, Phil."

"We can give it a try at least," he said, in an encouraging way. "Even if you only copy my letters for me, it will be a help. Come now, you have said you would like to give man's work a try. When will you have such a chance again?"

129

"Very well. I'll do it, if you both feel there is nothing scandalous in it."

"I had not thought that would deter you," he said, lifting a brow to level a bold look at me.

"Then you have not understood me very well," I returned.

"Scandalous? Pooh!" his sister scoffed, fearing I would dump myself back in her lap. "And we shan't tell anyone in any case. We'll say she is a house guest. That will prevent any talk," she averred to Philmot.

"Well, Miss Fenwick, what do you say?" he asked.

"I am game to give it a try. Let us see how it works out. If you feel I am not worth my hire, you can discharge me."

"Clap hands on a bargain," Lady Synge decreed, relief evident on every relaxed wrinkle of her face. We shook hands like a couple of gentlemen, and it was done.

"I shall go above and begin packing," I said, happy to have found a route out of my problem.

"I'll send a carriage around for your trunks," he offered. "When can I expect to see you report for work?"

"Right after lunch," I told him, hoping to catch Harmsworth during his morning visit.

I had a great deal to do. It was not possible to keep an eye peeled for Harmsworth, but when I asked Alice later, she told me he had not called. "Why do you ask?"

"He was going to bring me something. Will you have it sent over to Lord Philmot's place when it comes?"

"What is he going to bring?" she asked, bright with curiosity.

Unsure whether to expect bills or jingling coins, I hardly knew what to reply. "A letter—some information he is procuring for me," I answered, with a vague air.

"Very well."

I was off, with an assurance from Lady Synge that I would be hearing from her. She promised to keep me informed on Dottie's progress, which was a matter of real concern to me. I was becoming maternally fond of the child.

My spirits were high as I clipped along to Hanover Square. This job promised to be more interesting than overseeing the schoolroom. Neither did I think all my time would be occupied with work. A house guest I was posing as. Such a pose would demand social doings, would it not? An occasional party did not seem out of the question, or a drive in the park. I knew well enough Lord Philmot did not spend his every hour at labor. Quite the contrary. I tried not to be overly optimistic, but some feeling in my breast told me he had asked me to his home to become better acquainted with me. I knew there were hundreds of university-educated younger sons in the city who would have snapped at the chance of being his secretary. Working for a nobleman in such a capacity was one of the established ladders to fortune. Well, well, there was more than one way to climb a ladder, and for once, a woman was getting a toehold.

Chapter Thirteen

HIS HOME WAS ELEGANT in the extreme, larger than his sister's and better maintained. A butler showed me in, where I glimpsed off to my left a very large and richly appointed saloon. On the other side an open doorway showed a smaller parlor, also done up in the first style. A stairway in the distance gave a glimmer, no more, of additional fineries beyond, with gilt-framed portraits forming a chain up the wall. The butler took me right through to his lordship's study. This chamber was not so beautifully done, though it did not lack refinement. It was obviously a real working study. The desk dominated it, flanked on either side by straight-backed chairs. For himself, Philmot had a more comfortable seat, padded and armed, but not ornately carved. Around the walls were mahogany-fronted cabinets on which rested stacks of papers and books. Other than a fireplace, a table holding a carafe and glasses, there was not much in the way of creature comforts to be seen. From the three windows on the back wall there was a view of a small garden, a hedge, and a house rising beyond. Nothing to induce one to spend hours admiring the view.

"Miss Fenwick, punctual, as I might have expected," Philmot said, arising to greet me. He indicated one of the chairs with a flourish of a hand, and I sat down across from him.

"This seems a very efficient setup you have here," I complimented him.

"Harding, my last secretary, arranged it for me, carefully removing all distractions to force me to work. I fooled him, by hiring the most distracting secretary I could find."

The compliment, accompanied as it was by a bold smile, caused me a little worry. He had not been so obvious in his compliments at Russell Square. "Kind of you to say so. I thought it was my mind you had hired, not my face."

"I was not speaking of your face only, Miss Fenwick," he replied to that setdown, while his eyes toured to other aspects of my anatomy that appeared to please him. I had not come envisioning business only, but certainly a flirtation in such poor taste as this never once entered my mind.

I stirred restively in my chair, thinking how best to depress him. "Would you care to show me around the office?" I asked.

"I will be charmed to show you anything you wish to see." He arose, wearing a mocking smile, to walk out from behind his desk, offering me a hand up from the chair. When I was on my feet, the hand remained in mine. We turned towards one of the mahogany cabinets, he using the operation to lightly slide the arm around my waist. "In here you will find, if you are interested in such dull stuff, about two tons of paper dealing with the Corn Laws," he began.

"If it is your work, then of course I am interested."

"Is it only my *work* you are interested in, Miss Fenwick? There's a leveler for me."

"I *did* come here as a secretary, Philmot," I felt compelled to remind him.

He smiled a very knowing smile, and said absolutely nothing. He did not have to. It was all there to interpret from that bold, lazy, knowing smile. He thought I had come to make a play for him. The fact that I had did not enter into it; he had no way of knowing it. My pride was stung. He presumed a great deal to stand with his arm around me in this casual way, as though I were no better than a light-skirt. Was that what he thought of me?

I twitched away to the next cabinet. He was not two steps behind me. He placed one hand on the cabinet, the other soon found its way behind my back, with a little more pressure this time. "In here are my private documents. More interesting than the other, or so I am conceited enough to think."

It was my turn to say nothing. I walked on, but no matter where I walked, he was there behind me, seeming to crowd me to the wall. I could not go so far as to say he had seduction on his mind, but certainly he was up to mischief. When he began speaking in a significant way about his pleasure at my being a modern-minded, enlightened lady, I was less sure about the seduction. "I think it is time we get down to business, Philmot. That is why I am here," I said brusquely.

"I could not agree with you more, Olivia," he said, and yanked me into his arms. With no ceremony, no tenderness, no respect, with nothing but an excess of nerve and animal strength, he kissed me so hard my lips ached. The most humiliating thing of all was that there was not even any real passion in the embrace. I pushed him off and delivered such a sharp slap across his cheek he would not soon forget it.

"This is a strange reaction from a lady who gives lessons in sex," he said, his eyes wide with amazement. I had the infinite satisfaction of seeing the imprint of my hand turning to red on his cheek.

"I give lessons in health too, but I am not a doctor. I did not come here to be insulted." I turned on my heel and headed for the door, already wondering where the deuce I was to go. It was with relief I heard his steps coming after me, hastening to beat me to the door, and close it in my face.

"This has been a misunderstanding. I am sorry," he said, in a voice so far removed from either sorrow or humility it was difficult to believe his sincerity.

"I can't think what I have done to give rise to such a misunderstanding."

"Call it a *suspicion* then, if you dislike my choice of word. I suspected, when I heard of your secret assignations with a gentlemen of uncertain reputation . . ."

"There were no secret assignations. There was one accidental meeting and there was one arranged appointment for *Alice* to meet him, under my chaperonage. She was unable to come. As to his reputation, he is well enough thought of to be welcome at your sister's house."

"*I* warned you against him."

"A case of the pot calling the kettle black, it would seem."

"I have apologized. There is not the least necessity for you to go tearing from the house as though the hounds of hell were after you. You will not find me to persist where my attentions are so obviously not welcome."

I considered the apology in silence, undecided as to my course. "My suspicion was unfounded," he went on, in a conciliating vein. "I have embarrassed you, and myself. Let us forget it happened."

"How did you hear about my meeting Harmsworth?"

"Dottie told me about the first meeting. I learned of the other through a friend who chanced to see and recognize the two of you. Were there other encounters?"

"No. Did you tell Synge? Is that why he is in the boughs?"

"Certainly not. One does not relate *suspicions,* particularly about a lady's virtues, without some corroboration."

"I shouldn't think a *gentleman* would relate them at all."

"I did not say circulate. If founded, they obviously must be relayed if the lady in question has impressionable girls under her guardianship."

"So that's why you asked me here!" I'm sure my cheeks were crimson with shame. How had I been fool enough to think he was interested in marrying me?

"Are two apologies not sufficient? I am very relieved to be proven wrong. And I still require a secretary. You obviously came for that purpose. Let us get on with it."

He turned back to his desk, while I hesitated at the doorway, torn by the conflicting desires of leaving in a huff, to show my disgust, and running to the desk to get down to work. Such an interesting job was unlikely to come in my way again. There was, too, some desire to show him how far mistaken he had been in my character and conduct. He had apologized, and an apology did not come easy to him I think. I walked slowly back into the room and took up my position on the chair across from him. The thing might never have happened. His countenance was unperturbed as he leaned over a stack of papers roughly a foot high.

"I am fallen a little behind in my correspondence," he said. "I must go out soon, but shall give you some work to occupy your afternoon."

"Fine."

"These are arranged in chronological order. We'll just begin at the top and answer them." He lifted up one and perused it a moment. "This is from the Vechler Shipbuilding Company. Tell them no," he said, and set the sheet aside.

"No what?" I asked, amazed at this terse way of proceeding.

"The matter will explain itself to a bright lady like you. When you scan the letter, you will see they are trying to push additional shares of the company on me. I have put notes on these letters for you to look at. This one," he went on quickly, selecting the next, "you can tell them a hundred pounds and enclose a cheque. My bank book you will find there," he said, pointing to a leather case on the desk. "Make it out to Hanley and I'll sign."

"A hundred pounds for what?" I asked, my poor head spinning.

"The letter will explain," he said impatiently. "A connection of mine dunning me for a handout." It was laid aside. "This one is a no; this one a yes; this one tell them maybe in the summer . . ." He ran through about twenty letters, with only the scantiest remark about each. I hoped his notes were more informative.

Even during this brief interval, he kept glancing at his watch. Before half an hour was up, he arose to leave. "That should keep you busy till I get back. If you finish, you can begin to browse through my files of correspondence to get an idea how things go on. There is an address book in that cabinet," he said, pointing behind him. "If you have any questions, just jot them down and I'll explain when I get back. Sorry to have to rush so. If you would like to go up to your room to freshen up, I'll have the servants prepare your office."

While a dozen questions formed on my lips, he smiled and walked out. There was no lingering trace of anything but business. I went out into the hallway to see Philmot talking to the butler.

"Show Miss Fenwick to the Green Room, if you please," he said, touched his fingers to his curled beaver hat, and walked out.

"The Green? I thought ..." the butler said to his retreating form. It was to the Green Room I was taken, and it was no very grand affair either. In that mansion, I suspected it was especially set aside for the dunning connections such as Hanley. The servant had seemed uncertain as to taking me there, giving me a suspicion it was not the one originally intended for a more compliant Miss Fenwick. I was still hot with wrath at the memory of my reception belowstairs upon first entering the study. What would he have done had I gone along with his scheme? Had he intended discreetly keeping me as a mistress under his roof? I had thought they were kept in style at a good safe distance from the family abode. About the only aspect of it that did not gall was that at least a man's mistress was generally pretty. I hardly considered myself attractive enough to qualify in such a role.

My heart lifted somewhat as I descended the grand staircase. The butler awaited me below, to show me to my office. I felt very business-like as I gathered up the letters and address book. Philmot seemed to be well organized. I would show him I was not a whit less so. He had thrown a great deal at my head in one lump, but the letters and his notes would explain. As for the rest, why it was only to write out a neat, grammatical reply. I went towards my office, stopping at the doorway to note it was by no means so gracious as his lordship's. Even the word plain was not too strong. There was a deal table, a straight, hard chair, no fireplace, one window that gave a stunning view of a downspout and the corner of the back doorstoop, and three curved brass hooks on the wall.

I was disappointed, but there was no one to complain to, so instead I settled down to business. I judged I had four hours before I would have to begin dressing for dinner. I intended to have the assigned work completed. It was not exactly interesting, though I was surprised to discover in how many commercial affairs he dabbled. Of more interest were the family matters; the number of relatives who found occasion to ask his help, either financial or to find a home or position for some wanting member. The letters were of all tones—an Aunt Martha wrote in great detail about the family, a Cousin Alfred came close to demanding his lordship's intercession to find a post in London, another had a friend who wished to know if there were any country livings going. Some just plain asked for money. The replies varied as much as the requests. In some cases there was a scribbled yes or no on the margin, and nothing else to tell me what tone to adopt. I followed the clue given in each missive. The chatty Aunt Martha got a polite answer and fifty pounds. Cousin Alfred was invited to present himself in person and outline his skills, talents, and so on.

After a few hours, my neck was cramped, my feet asleep, my fingers sore from the close work. I walked about to rest my eyes and stretch my limbs. From the hallway the sounds of tinkling glasses and feminine laughter floated towards me. The maiden-aunt chaperone entertaining. I could hardly go uninvited to her party, but I could at least have a cup of tea. When it was brought, there was no room for it on my paper-littered desk. I requested a small table to be brought to my room.

The servant, a junior footman, was polite and friendly. When he asked if there was anything else I required, and said his lordship had asked that I be taken care of, I took advantage of the offer. "Do you think you could find me a more comfortable chair? This one is very hard."

He was soon back with a nice padded one, which was unfortunately too low to suit the desk, but it was retained for my tea break. As I sipped, it struck me the room was so spartan as to be unpleasant. No pictures on the wall, nothing but a linoleum on the floor. One could only wonder at this evidence of skimpiness in such a rich household. "Lord Philmot's last secretary was no hedonist, was he?" I asked, with a disparaging look around at the surroundings.

"Oh this is not the secretary's office, Ma'am. This is just a storage room that was cleared out recently to make room for old files."

"I think I have been put in the wrong room," I said, sure it must be the case.

"No, Ma'am. His lordship particularly said to put you in this cupboard. Mr. Harding left some personal effects in his office which he'll be picking up soon."

The idea was not slow in occurring to me that I had been put in this cupboard, aptly described, to be as uncomfortable as possible. Philmot had not liked having to apologize, or perhaps it was having his advances repulsed that had decided him to behave in this way. I finished my tea and returned to work. Compared to my teaching chores, this was slave labor. No one to talk to, no pretty surroundings, nothing but slogging through letters, first figuring out what they were about, then deciphering Philmot's scrawls with regard to an answer, then to compose the reply in some tone that was appropriate.

I was more than ready for my dinner. This at least would be a relaxing, civilized interlude in a dull, hard day. I would wear my blue silk. I wondered if there would be, company for dinner. He had not said so. Indeed he had not said I would dine at the family table, but as I was to be called a guest outside of the walls, I could hardly be fed in the kitchen. My head ached when I finished the last letter, but I revived somewhat when I placed the neat stack on his desk. I felt he would be hard pressed to complain of his bargain. A man could not have done a better day's work, I thought, with a sense of satisfaction at a job well done.

After making a toilette grand enough to do justice to whomever sat at the table, I went belowstairs, to find Philmot was dining out—had already left, and I was to take my meal with his Aunt Marion, whose presence was to guarantee propriety to my working visit. I cannot imagine why he tolerated this female presence in his household. She was of that baneful species, the maiden aunt. Miss Millichope was her name. She was an imposing dame of statuesque proportions. Her gray hair was worn in a fringe across a broad brow. The cheekbones were broad, the eyes a pale blue, the nose childishly small and upturned. She wore a rose crepe gown of excellent cut, whose excellence by no means concealed her large size. When she spoke, she lifted her brows and looked down that tiny nose, as though assessing a particularly loathsome specimen from the lower animal kingdom. She wheezed when she spoke, as though the exertion caused her unsuspected effort.

"You would be the gel helping Philmot with his letters," she told me, after I had curtsied and gave her my name. "Peculiar way of carrying on, but he tells me you are clever, Miss Fenwick."

"Kind of him to say."

"Yes." She wheezed again while surveying me for some seconds, then lifted one languorous hand to indicate I might be seated on a chair across from her. "You are one of these modern gels who reads and all that," was her next charge against me.

"I enjoy reading," I confessed.

"So do I. The young think they have discovered everything. I read a great deal in my youth. I would read still, but for the trouble with my eyes. Everything blurs after a while. It is likely a result of all the heavy reading of my youth."

"How very unfortunate."

"Not a complete misfortune. I have read everything worth reading. Now, in my more mature years, it is my intention to digest it, and to contemplate philosophy. Do you read philosophy?"

"A little."

There was another of the painful wheezes, louder than any that had preceded it. The brows, tired of resting so high on her forehead, lowered, leaving behind deep lines. "You want to read Locke," she advised me. "There is a deal of common sense in Locke. Hobbes ought to be banned. And what is your opinion of Mr. Godwin?" was her next question. She had been warned of me. I disclaimed all support of the wicked Godwin.

"The likes of him are turning the world upside down," she cautioned. "In *my* day gels were told where to marry. They made good marriages of convenience and had affairs of the heart. Nowadays the ladies marry for love and have affairs of convenience. One hardly knows which is worse. It is why I never married. Philmot tells me we have that view in common."

I disliked to admit holding any view in common with this one, but told her I did not view matrimony as the only style of life for a lady. "An independent life is not for everyone," she told me, "but for those of us with fortitude and spirit, it is possible."

During the long meal, she told me a great many things. She informed me which authors, artists, architects and composers I ought to admire. She informed me any poetry written in this century was pernicious and ought to be burned. She explained in minute and totally incomprehensible detail why it was impossible for anyone with a logical mind to learn French. If they persisted in flying in the face of nature, they would eventually cause absolute deterioration of the mental faculties. French was held accountable for many of the modern world's ills. I never listened to so much rubbish in my life, and to cap it all off, at the meal's end she told me she was very pleased with me, and was sure we would be great friends as we thought so much alike. I had been too preoccupied to offer her any worthy contradictions.

I did not anticipate an entire evening in her company with any great relish. This ordeal was spared me. She was going to hear a concert of antique music with some friends. "I know you will be occupied, for Philmot said you would not likely get around to his accounting till after dinner."

I had done more than enough work for one day. After Miss Millichope had left, I went back to my office to think of ways of making it more comfortable. Before long, I went to take a peek at Mr. Harding's room. It was much finer than the cupboard in which I was expected to slave. It was a miniature of Philmot's own room. If the last secretary had left any personal items behind him, they were small enough to have been contained in the drawers of the desk. It was a weak excuse to put me in the closet. I opened the drawers to see a few papers and books, enough to fill a small carton, which they were soon doing.

In the morning I would tell Philmot the real office was now empty, and ask if there was a particular reason why he wished to keep me in the cubbyhole. I would be interested to hear his answer. The remainder of the evening was spent in my chamber, fixing it to my liking. I found time to worry at Harmsworth's not showing up with my money. With luck, he would come when Philmot was out. It would be uncomfortable to meet with him after the recent altercation between Philmot and myself, but one meeting was essential. I must get my money and my ticket to redeem the diamonds.

Chapter Fourteen

NO HOUR HAD BEEN mentioned as the one for beginning work in the morning. I went to breakfast at eight thirty and ate alone. Before nine, I was back in my office. While awaiting Philmot's arrival, I began browsing through the files of correspondence, as he had suggested. At nine thirty, he came in. I showed him the pile of answered letters. He sat down to read them through quickly, with no complaints and no praise. "If you'll seal these up as I sign them, I can frank them now and have done with it," he said, in a businesslike manner. This busy interval left little time for talk, but he did say Miss Millichope had expressed approval of me.

I was not at home enough to venture any derogatory remark. "She tells me we have some things in common," I replied vaguely.

"I thought you two would hit it off," he said. "You always reminded me of Aunt Marion. How she must have been in her younger years, I mean," he added.

I was hardly more offended than shocked. How was it possible anyone saw a resemblance to *me* in that opinionated, foolish, fat woman? I sensed that, like my cubbyhole, it was intended as a slight to my esteem, a revenge for having put down his advances. I folded the letters in silence, refusing to rise to his bait. This done, we dealt with the morning's mail. "In future you could open the letters before I arrive," he mentioned, "to save me some time."

My plan of coming to the office at nine thirty evaporated. The preceding day's performance with the letters was repeated. They were run through rapidly, with directions for replying to each briefly noted. "I shall be out all day," he said when we were finished. "If you get time, you could work on the accounts this afternoon. See if you can balance up my book. Nothing has been done to it since Harding left. It's probably in a mess. There is a list of some cheques I have written somewhere." He routed around in drawers, finally producing a scribbled sheet, very long, of sums spent. I was curious to get a look at it.

The whole of his work took about an hour. By ten thirty, he was arising from his desk, his day's duty done. "If there are any questions, just ask. I hope you are quite comfortable? I told the servants to see to your needs."

"There is one point, Lord Philmot. Is there any reason I cannot use Harding's office? The cupboard you had cleared out for me is cramped and uncomfortable. Warm in this season, you know."

"Unfortunately, Harding left his things . . ."

"His papers and books have been put into a carton. I had some time left over after answering those few letters you gave me yesterday."

"Oh," was all he said. "In that case there is no reason you should not use the room. I am happy to see you are making yourself at home, Ma'am. If you require anything else, I'm sure you'll see to getting it for yourself." The tone was similar to the words—ambiguous, but certainly capable of being interpreted as pushiness on my part.

"Thank you. I dislike to bother you for every detail, for I can see you are busy."

"I have a bill being debated in the House, and without Harding to help me, I must do all that work myself. Now that we are getting caught up on this backlog, perhaps you will find time to give me a hand with my political work."

I could not foresee a single second free that day, so made no offer. All morning I read and wrote, while the ink seeped onto my fingers, destroying the white cuffs of my morning gown. Even Miss Millichope was out for luncheon. I ate alone from a tray in the office, feeling I had struck a poor bargain to have come here and be treated like a slave. When the servant came to remove my tray, he handed me a letter. It was heavy, encouraging me to believe Harmsworth had been to call. "A gentleman left this for you," he said.

"In future, I would like to be told when I have callers," I informed him. I was relieved this particular one had come during his lordship's absence.

"Mr. Harding never had callers when he was working," the footman told me, but in an apologetic manner, as one explaining a lapse.

"I do not expect to have many, but if anyone comes for me, I would like to be told. Thank you."

When he left, I eagerly tore open the letter, the thought forming that I might take the money and leave Philmot's house. Really it was inhumane the way I was being treated here. Oh, but my treatment at Harmsworth's hands was worse! The wretched man had settled for thirty guineas for my diamonds, and then he forgot to include the chit that would allow me to redeem them when I had received my salary. He did not even mention the name of the dealer with whom he had left them. I was in a horrible quandary, for it was unlikely I would be running into Harmsworth again for an age. I had no notion where he resided either, to send him a note, and could hardly enquire of Philmot for the information.

I was happier than I ever thought I would be to see Lady Synge, when she dropped around that afternoon. My first question must be for Dottie's progress. When I heard she was coming along satisfactorily, I asked for Alice, which led easily to enquire whether Harmsworth was still amongst her court, and where he lived. I learned he had rooms at Alvanley, a superior residence where many gentlemen hired rooms. "He is certainly on the verge of offering for Alice. I hope the silly chit has the wit to accept. He is riddled with duns at the moment, poor soul, but will be coming into I don't know how many thousands when his uncle dies. She shall not be allowed to accept her captain if *I* know anything. Enough about her. She gives me the migraine ten times a day with her stupid behavior. I wish I had hired you last year, Miss Fenwick. How does this job you are undertaking for Philmot go on?"

"Very interesting," I lied, brightly.

"You'll not want to come back to us. Quite a holiday you are having," she answered merrily. "Your own pretty office, just like a lady of business." After a fifteen minutes' chat, during which I felt I ought to be back at my work, she arose to go.

"Here are Philmot's invitations for Alice's ball—his and Marion's, and of course your own, Miss Fenwick," she said, handing me the white squares. "You will not want to miss it. You may be back with us by then, for Dottie will be recovered before the date, but I brought it along with the others."

I thanked her very heartily, and felt a pang of lonesomeness when she left. Was it possible I was coming to *like* Lady Synge? I liked her better than Miss Millichope in any case. If she was an ignoramus, she at least did not put on the air of being blue.

The days unrolled at Lord Philmot's home, the one not much different from another. My unwilling body became accustomed to sitting for hours at a stretch, cramped over a desk. Of course there were breaks in the monotony. Callers came, and if Philmot was out, I had sometimes to deal with them personally, following my employer's instructions if the call was anticipated, and improvising when it was not. I received no complaints for my work, never a word of reprimand, and never one of praise. He was determined to treat me as if I were a male secretary. My being more ornamental than Harding was not referred to again. Had I had to look forward to a lifetime of such drudgery, I would have revolted, but it was for only two weeks, and already one was up. I could take another week without breaking.

I had an answer to my note to Harmsworth, enclosing the pawn shop ticket and explaining that thirty guineas was the highest the man would go. As I needed the money, he thought it best to take what he could get. I disliked it, but accepted it.

With the correspondence caught up, there was less letter writing to be done. Philmot gave me some government reports to read and summarize, but this was not a success. I could make neither head nor tail of the jargon those learned gentlemen employed, and told Philmot so. "It is half Latin and half nonsense," I told him.

"Have we reached the boundaries of your competence so soon?" he asked, smiling with glee. "Strange, I seem to remember hearing you bruited as a particular dab in politics."

"An interested observer only, Sir. I make no claim to comprehending the incomprehensible. It seems to me they obscure their meaning unnecessarily in a sea of heretofores and provisos. It is as bad a jumble as philosophy."

"No lover of philosophy either, Miss Fenwick? My aunt will be disappointed in you. Has she not recommended you look into Locke?"

"She has given me Locke to peruse in my *spare time,* of which I do not have very much."

"Harding usually managed a couple of hours off every afternoon, and *he* handled a good deal of government work for me as well."

"You were unfortunate to have lost such a prodigy."

"He had too good a brain to waste in being a mere copier of letters."

Perhaps this was not intended as an insult, but it was not difficult to read into one. "Have you any more letters for me to copy?" I asked with a pointed stare.

Without batting an eyelash, he turned to his correspondence and handed me a pile.

I eventually got around to the account books. A major tally had not been taken since Harding's departure. It was a revealing job, to see what sums of money poured into his pockets. The annual rental from his tenant farms was not the half of it. He had stacks of consols, collecting their five percent, shares in manufacturing companies, houses and commercial buildings all over London. The flow of monies going out was also high. He lived not only well but extravagantly. To do the man justice, I must admit large sums were given to charity and poor relations. Not less than four male cousins were being schooled at his expense, while several female relations received pensions as well.

The name of Lady Beaton was recognized as being amongst his beneficiaries. It occurred to me she lived high on the hog for a woman with no apparent fortune of her own. Though her address was Upper Grosvenor Square, the home had been substantial, and of course I knew she had traded her tilbury up for a phaeton, which indicated she was not an elderly female. On one occasion I opened one of her letters and was taken to task for it, though I had been told to open his post to save him time.

Her note did not arrive with the regular post, but was brought by a footman with the message that it was urgent. Philmot was out for the day. Whether he would be home for dinner was a moot point. This being the case, I tore open the message myself and read it. It was a plea for funds, couched in such terms as left no doubt as to the urgency of the matter. The bailiff was even then in her saloon demanding payment of two hundred pounds for "those items he suggested she purchase from Rundell and Bridges." This establishment dealt in silver and jewels, which told me the purchase was an extravagance for a lady on the dole, but as Philmot had suggested it, it sounded as though he intended to pay. Perplexed, I stood contemplating what to do. There was no way of being in touch with him and no way of writing her a cheque without his signature. I took the decision to pilfer the cash box, which he kept in his desk for such emergencies. It usually contained about twice the sum asked for. I sent Lady Beaton a note explaining the situation, and enclosing the money. Of course I told him about it when he returned to change for dinner. I saw at once by his stiff face he was angry.

"I prefer to handle my personal correspondence myself," he said.

"The messenger said it was most urgent, and indeed when I read the bailiff . . ."

"Yes, I understand, but in future any messages from Lady Beaton, however urgent, will please be held for me to open. Under no circumstance do I want you disbursing money without my authority. There would be too many ready to take advantage of your inexperience," he added as a palliative.

"You always pay her bills." I pointed out. "Should I not have given her the money?"

He directed a look on me that could have pierced iron, so concentrated was it. Then he suddenly shrugged his shoulders and gave an indulgent laugh. "It hardly matters. Kate would have got it by hook or by crook. She always does."

"She is an extravagant lady, buying herself trinkets at Rundell and Bridges, when it is you who must foot the bill. I think you should exercise a tighter rein on your expensive relations."

The indulgent smile faded. A snowflake on a hot iron would not have vanished faster. I had presumed too far to criticize one of his relations, or himself. "I am not one of your schoolgirls to be instructed, Ma'am. Lady Beaton happens to have particular claims on me," he condescended to add, before he turned sharply aside to look over some letters I had ready for him. "That will be all, Miss Fenwick," he said, without looking up again.

I left to change for dinner, but the matter continued to nag at me. I knew from his accounts he gave the woman large sums of money, larger than to most his hangers on. Her home, for instance, belonged to him and was used without paying rent. She had a boy enrolled at Eton for whom Philmot paid the bill. She had a regular allowance from him, not terribly large, but considering the other perquisites, it was more than adequate for a life of elegance. Knowing nothing of her, it was easy to imagine her with some peculiar claims on him, some favor rendered in the past, or some fall of bad luck that evoked his sympathy. My interest in her stemmed from my having purchased her tilbury and seen her home, perhaps. I had not even that much to do with most of these anonymous relatives with whom I corresponded.

Philmot dined at home that evening, as he occasionally did. I may have imagined it, but I thought his mood was softening somewhat. We had a lively discussion of poetry over our meal, with himself taking up the cudgel on behalf of the moderns, while I defended the oldsters. As Miss Millichope's eyes had given out on her before the advent onto the scene of such rebels as Byron and Keats, she roundly condemned them without benefit of a trial. I thought Philmot might remain at home that evening, but he went out, as usual.

Chapter Fifteen

WITH THE EXCUSE THAT governmental duties kept him busy, Philmot shoved his social correspondence onto my shoulders, along with my other work. I answered his invitations, and when he decided to have a party himself, I was asked to write out the cards, from a list handed me by Miss Millichope. Her eyes again were held to be the excuse, though she did in fact read for hours a day at trashy magazines and novels. She was as lazy as a hound dog. Philmot returned one afternoon early to inform us of the party. I had mixed emotions, liking the idea of meeting some people, but not caring to hear that its preparations, to some extent, would be my chore.

"You will see to arranging for flowers and food, Miss Fenwick?" he asked, with some inflection that made it a question about whose answer there was no doubt. "I always tend to the wine myself."

"How grand a do will it be?" I asked, to gain an idea what quantity of food and flowers were involved.

"A small party. Auntie will give you the list, and you

can deal accordingly. Harding had a list of merchants he dealt with for these affairs. I'll see if I can find it."

I had arranged many small afternoon parties for my father at Bath, and saw no difficulty in doing another. After he left and Miss Millichope found her list, I learned his idea of a small party was over a hundred guests! I was in a complete dither, but not about to admit it after certain aspersions already cast on my managing a grand household, while I was at Synges. He found Harding's book and gave it to me. With this aid, the job became less impossible. Gunter, the pastry cook, Holbein, the florist, and several other tradesmen were sent for to consult with and take orders. From them, I learned indirectly how his lordship liked a party done up. In the first style was how. It would put a good dent in his pocketbook, but I cared nothing for that.

Two days before the party, the florist brought arranged baskets of blooms to the house. I was engaged in placing them about the saloons when I at last made the acquaintance of Lady Beaton. I had been busy all morning consulting with the servants on the minutiae of the party. The butler stood with me in a small parlor, exclaiming over the arrangements. "This seems very expensive," I said to Holbein, tallying up his figures. "We are using our own palm trees for the corners, you recall."

Before he answered, the housekeeper came in. "Miss Fenwick," she began.

Busy as I was, I called over my shoulder without looking, "Just leave the list there, Mrs. Rogers. I'll see to it in a minute." She was to bring me a list of the servants and their specific functions at the do, so that no detail would be overlooked.

"It's company, Ma'am," she said. I turned to see standing beside her the most exquisite creature ever

154

seen outside of a frame. She was a Gainsborough lady come to life, with the skin of that incredible translucent quality, as though light shone from somewhere within her. She was tall, willowy, draped all in a dusty blue color from head to toe. She wore a small turban, the headgear more usually assigned to aging females. How very well it showed off her oval-shaped face. There was nothing to detract from the exquisite planes of the cheeks and nose. I wondered that more young ladies were not pushing their curls up out of sight. Certainly it darted into my head to do so, a soon as I got up to my room. The edges of her pelisse were trimmed in narrow swathes of some fur that had been dyed to match the outfit. Even her reticule and shoes were blue, the whole orchestrated to blend with a patterned gown in blue and white that peeped out beneath the pelisse. She smiled, a somewhat icy smile, and said in a world-weary voice, "Miss Fenwick, I presume?"

"Lady Beaton," the housekeeper informed me.

"Lady Beaton!" I exclaimed involuntarily, in a more surprised tone that I had intended employing.

"Your surprise is not greater than my own," she replied, regarding me with an assessing glance. "Philmot did not tell me you were turned housewife, to oversee his domestic arrangements. A woman to write up some letters for him is what he said."

"Wait for me. I'll be right back," I said to the man from the florist, then turned again to Lady Beaton, wondering what in the world to do with her. Miss Millichope was out, or I would have turned the caller over to her.

"Lord Philmot is not in," I said, as we walked into the hallway. "Nor his aunt either. Could I take some message for you?"

"I did not come to see Phil or Marion," she answered, turning towards the front of the house. I followed along, full of curiosity to hear why she had come. "I came to see *you*," she told me.

"Oh," I said, with a great lack of ingenuity. We turned left into a small parlor, sat down like any two ladies contemplating a pleasant visit.

She examined me a moment in a haughty way, then gave her decision. "You are not what I expected."

"Am I not? I must confess I had formed a different picture of you as well. I had no idea you would be so beautiful."

She recognized the compliment by a barely visible nod of the head. "What has Philmot told you about me?" she asked.

"Very little. I bought your tilbury from you, if you will recall. That is how I come to know your name. And of course from your letter . . ."

"I see." She leaned back, her elbow on the arm of the sofa, and went on regarding me, staring boldly in a manner never adopted by any lady to her equal. "Just exactly what is your position here, Miss Fenwick?" she condescended to enquire when she was done looking.

I adopted her own trick of the bold stare. "I am a house guest, Lady Beaton. As Lord Philmot's secretary has left suddenly, I am doing a little correspondence for him. Are there any more questions?"

"A great many, my dear, but I think I would prefer to put them to Phil. It seems to me you were not engaged in correspondence when I arrived, but in running the house."

"Just helping out with the arrangements for the party."

"What party?" she asked sharply.

My mind went spinning back to the list, to determine whether her name had been on it. I could not recall addressing a card for her, but it was odd her name had been omitted. Surely she, a close connection of the family, ought to have been included. It was easy to believe Miss Millichope, not a keen worker, had overlooked it. "An afternoon party," I said.

"When is this great do to occur?"

"The day after tomorrow."

There was a glow in her eyes, half malevolence, half intrigue. She made no mention of a card, nor did I volunteer any reason for the omission. She sat a moment thinking in silence, then arose suddenly. She reached into her reticule and handed me a letter. "Please give this to Philmot," she said in a bright, offhand way. "It is *personal*, Miss Fenwick. Philmot likes to handle his personal correspondence himself, I believe? I expect we shall meet again soon."

I understood all her insinuations. I accepted the letter and followed her out, without speech. "How is my old tilbury holding together?" she asked, to give an appearance to the servants of civility.

"Fine. I am happy with it."

"Too old-fashioned for me, I am afraid. We are all driving high perch phaetons nowadays, Miss Fenwick. If you wish to be in style, you must have Philmot buy you one."

"I buy my own things, Ma'am," I told her.

"Ah—did I say *buy?* I meant *find,* of course." A trill of laughter wafted back over her shoulder as she was shown out.

When I returned to the flower arranging, my mind was only half on it. My curiosity was burning to know what was in that letter, but I could not open it. I stuck it into the pocket of my skirt, and went on with my work. About ten minutes later, I noticed the odor of musk that followed me everywhere. Even above the scent of the flowers it was evident. I soon realized it came from my pocket.

When Philmot returned, he came to look in on his party arrangements. "Any difficulty?" he asked.

"Not at all. Lady Beaton was here during your absence," I said.

"She came *here?*" he asked, staring.

"Why yes. Is there some reason why she should not? I thought she must have been here any number of times."

"No, she has never been here," he answered.

It was difficult indeed to know why he should be angry. He looked at me in a peculiar way. Had I not known him better, I would have said he looked almost apologetic. "What did she want?" he asked.

I handed him the letter. "She said she wanted to see *me*, but all she did was to give me this letter for you. She uses a very strong scent, does she not?"

"Yes, too strong," he agreed, looking with noticeable distaste at the letter.

I smiled to see him so vexed. "What's the matter, Philmot? Afraid she wants another two hundred pounds?" I asked, teasing him, as he was in an approachable mood. I felt strangely relieved myself. I had some feeling, when I found her to be such an Incomparable, that there might be some romance between her and Philmot, in whom I still had some proprietary interest. The matter was perfectly clear to me now. The obvious answer was that the lady was chasing after him, but his scowls as he looked at the letter told me how slight were her chances of success.

"Probably," he admitted, with a rueful smile.

"While we are on the subject of Lady Beaton, I must tell you I am in a bit of a pickle. It seems her name was not on the invitation list, and I am wondering whether I ought to send her a card. Your mentioning she has never been here. . . ."

"No," he said, very quickly, very firmly. "No, Kate would not enjoy the do."

I think Kate would have enjoyed it very much, but what he meant of course was that he would not enjoy to have her here. I was forming the idea Lady Beaton was not quite the thing. Her manners were somewhat ragged, to be sure. An impoverished widow, living on the fringes of society—very likely she was on the lookout for a patron, for if it were a husband she was after, I do not think she would have been excluded from Philmot's exclusive circle.

I was curious enough that I broached her name to Miss Millichope on the next occasion we were alone together. "Lady Beaton was here this afternoon," I mentioned in a casual way. "Your nephew seemed upset by the visit."

"Lady Beaton?" she asked, frowning. "I don't know any Lady Beaton, Miss Fenwick. What is she like?"

"Why, she is some connection of the family. A young widow—very pretty."

"We are no kin to the Beatons," she told me. "But a widow—I would know her maiden name, no doubt. You don't know what she was called before her marriage?"

"No, I don't. Kate is her first name."

"Kate," she said pensively, her broad brow creasing. "I don't know who she could be. I used to know all the cousins and nieces and nephews, but as I grow older, I forget everything. I used to know the first two chapters of my brother's Latin text by heart."

When she made these foolish assertions, I could not but remember Philmot's saying I reminded him of her, and be angry. What on earth could be the point of her having memorized two chapters of Latin? "Everyone was very impressed at my knowledge," she went on, with no consciousness of revealing her stupid vanity. "My friends were used to say I should have been a man, for when I was younger I was ready to tackle anything." At the moment, she was tackling a cup of tea

159

and a broadsheet picked up during her outing. The subject matter of the latter had to do with a sensational crime of passion that was widely read by the lower orders.

"Had I been twenty years younger, Miss Fenwick," she assured me, "you would not have had to come and help Philmot. I would have done it for him, but I am too old now for that hard work."

"The work is not hard, Ma'am, only tedious."

"I would not have liked that, for I always preferred a hard mental challenge," she said complacently, setting aside the broadsheet to pick up an old chapbook of Dicey's to try her brain. She had a collection of these. I had not seen them in ten years, and had never before in my life seen one in a polite saloon, but only in maid's rooms and such places. I picked up another that lay on the table. As I flipped through it, I saw it consisted of many crudely executed woodcuts and a minimum of actual print. "The Intriguing Wife and the Sharping Gallant" was the longest story in the book. The rest was filled in with ballads and childish sermons. I was too tired after my deal of real labor to arise and find something more interesting. As Miss Millichope was by this time deeply into hers, I sat perforce glancing through mine.

We were together, our heads bent over the books, when Lord Philmot came in, returned early from a dinner party. "The picture of domestic bliss," he said, smiling from the doorway. "My two blue ladies studying their Latin and literature. What is it you are reading, ladies?"

I positively blushed to be caught out at such a low pastime. Miss Millichope was too engrossed in her story to be interrupted. "I was just glancing at this little antique book your aunt was showing me," I replied, trying to maintain my dignity. "Interesting to

160

see how tastes have changed." I lay it aside, as far from his view as possible.

He advanced to the table, and with innate perversity picked it up to flip through. "I do not see that tastes have changed much," he disagreed, with a mocking look. "I make sure Alice would like this very much. I must confess, though, I had thought Miss Fenwick would be better employed."

"I am not reading this! Just glancing at it. It is always of interest to know what was read and enjoyed in the past," I pointed out.

"Not so very different from the thing Alice was reading the other week. *The Monk,* was it not?"

"She did not get it from *me.* I do not consider *The Monk* a suitable literary diversion for young ladies. A depraved cleric who carries on with wantons and his penitents and ultimately strikes a bargain with Satan himself is not what was considered suitable when *I* was in the schoolroom."

"You achieved this familiarity with the book after you were out of it then, and your taste already formed, I must conclude. Unless, of course, you are so superficial as to judge by hearsay."

"I usually know what I am talking about before I venture an opinion."

"Except, of course, on Vanbrugh," he pointed out, with a superior smile. "I have kept you unconscionably busy, I know, but thought the redoubtable Miss Fenwick would have discovered her way to my library before this time. If it is the fact of its being adjacent to my bedchamber that has kept you out, let me assure you there is no adjoining door. Merely I found I had need of more rooms downstairs, and more than enough bedchambers. I like to have my books near me at night, when I do most of my reading. I thought I would encounter you there some evening."

"I am usually asleep well before three or four," I replied, to let him know I was aware of his late hours.

"All that beauty sleep would account for your bright eyes and pink cheeks. Come, I shall show you where it is. In future, you will have more free time to indulge your taste for chapbooks. We are well caught up on business."

I looked to Miss Millichope, to excuse myself. She was deep into her tome, her face wearing a fatuous smile. Peering over her shoulder, Philmot read, " 'The Landlord Well Paid by the Handsome Tenant.' One of her favorites. We shan't disturb her." He offered his hand to help me arise.

As we went towards the stairway, I said, "I suppose you are on your way to some ball or rout party?"

"Gadfly that I am!" he agreed, with a *tsk*. "The fact is, I have been trotting too hard, and am on my way to bed. My friends at dinner this evening were kind enough to tell me I looked burned to the socket. Even gentlemen need their beauty sleep, you must know."

"Surely you are not going to bed at nine thirty!"

"I am, unless you have something better to suggest. Some nice quiet pastime it must be, Miss Fenwick. I am practically an invalid. The wretched truth of the matter is, I had a few rounds with Jackson this afternoon, and got hit such a blow in the liver I nearly collapsed."

"I wish I might have seen that!" I said, and meant it too.

"You still harbor some resentment of my *abominable* behavior the day you came here. You must at least give me credit for improvement. I have not backed you into any dark corners for an age. It took some self control too, I can tell you," he added, with a smile, to show he was joking.

"I trust your library is well lit, Sir?"

"It always was at night when Harding was with me, for he spent his time there. As Miss Fenwick has not even *discovered* the room, however, I cannot vouch for it."

"Oh Harding! I am coming to dislike him nearly as much as. . . . He was clearly a paragon. I do not hope to match Harding in anything."

"You are much prettier," he said with a bow.

I accepted the compliment with a curtsey and we proceeded into the library (well lit). Four walls were lined with shelves, the shelves lined with books. There was a long table with a dozen chairs in the middle of the room, but no free standing stacks. The shelves had that untidy look that hinted at their being used often, with gaps here and there where a book was out. "Yours are not so carefully arranged as your sister's. You have got the browns and blues and reds all mixed up." I quizzed him.

He threw back his head and laughed. "You discovered her trick! A marvelous touch, don't you think? We know *someone* who judges a book by its cover, eh Miss Fenwick?" he said, leaning his head close to mine.

"Someone other than myself, you infer?"

"You are sensitive. The greater part of my books are at my country place. I don't have time for any serious study when I am in London. You will find the left wall useless for your purposes. It is made up of books pertaining to my work in Government. The chapbooks are . . ."

"I read something other than chapbooks. I notice how well you are supplied with marble covers. They will be blamed on your mama, I daresay. You can no longer pass Miss Millichope, who reminds you so forcibly of myself, off as an intellectual who reads gothic tales. We have her number."

"Lady Synge is the culprit. She would have frisked

them off to Russell Square, but they did not match her decor. I must confess I took some pleasure from *The Monk* and *The Castle of Otranto* in my youth. Walpole was a friend of the family. Of course I more usually read . . ."

"Yes, of course. You would much prefer to read Philosophy, in Latin or German if you could find it," I told him.

"Let us concede between us we would each prefer Metaphysics to anything else ever written, but as we have it all off by heart, we shall put ourselves to sleep with a good novel. Just this one time, of course! We shan't repeat the vice till tomorrow night."

After we had each made our selection, carefully looking to see what the other had chosen and confirm it was nothing else but escape reading, we turned to leave. I wondered whether he would revert again to some quiet pastime for an hour before retiring. Cards or chess occurred as likely amusements, at either of which I might acquit myself passably. I did not intend to raise the matter if he did not, however.

"Did you happen to mention to Lady Beaton the day and hour of the party?" he asked suddenly.

"I believe she asked the *day* of it, and I told her. Not the hour. Are you set against her coming?"

The question seemed to surprise him. His brows lifted in astonishment, but his reply was not informative. "I prefer to *invite* folks to my home when I wish to entertain them."

"You can hardly turn her from the door. A relative of your family."

"A connection only," he replied.

A connection would imply she had married a relative, but Miss Millichope had already denied this. I sensed he disliked Lady Beaton, but could not imagine why he was so generous to her, if that were the case. "Perhaps she won't come," I said.

"Probably not," he agreed. Until the subject of Lady Beaton had arisen, we were going on famously. Such interchanges as this had been foreseen by me when I agreed to come. They had been delayed by his perfectly wretched behavior on the first day, but gradually the resentment on both sides had dissipated. "Well, I am for bed," he said, hefting the book and looking at it.

"I feel a little tired myself," I said, to hide my disappointment at the loss of further doings that night.

"I have worked you too hard. You should go out more."

"I have my tilbury. I could . . ."

"No!"

"I don't *always* drive into a ditch, Philmot!" I said, thinking he objected on that ground.

"I would like you to drive with me, tomorrow."

I was flattered, yet his objection had been rather violent. I was left with the distinct impression he did not wish me to drive in my tilbury, which was very odd, considering it was himself who had led me to buy it. "We'll arrange the time tomorrow morning. Goodnight."

He turned towards his room, and I turned down the hall towards my own, curious as to why he was so much friendlier than before, and a good deal more curious about Lady Beaton.

Chapter Sixteen

PHILMOT'S EARLY NIGHT DID him a world of good. He was in his office the next morning before I was, myself, and had already opened his mail. "Nothing of any importance," he told me, handing me four or five letters. I took them into my office, which I had spruced up slightly since taking over occupancy. I had formed the habit of snitching a few flowers when they came in and arranging myself a small bouquet. The picture of some ancient king standing in ermine robes with a staff in his hand had been hidden behind the desk and replaced with a French country scene purloined by a willing footman from a room seldom used abovestairs. A few of my own favorite bibelots brought from Synges rested on top of a cabinet. The door adjoining Philmot's office was left open, for he was so seldom in the room I kept an eye on it. Visitors, for instance, would enter there, and if I could not see them, they might leave unattended.

I sat down to answer the letters, thinking I would be finished inside of an hour, and have time to see the housekeeper and butler about the party the next afternoon. I noticed a couple of times Philmot was not at his desk, but standing near the window, looking out, apparently thinking about something. Twice when I looked up, he had turned to look through the door at me. It is disconcerting to think you are being watched as you go about your business. I decided to close the door, and in order to do it without seeming to resent his watching, I made the excuse of requiring the address book, carefully closing the door after me.

I had scarcely resumed my seat when the door opened and Philmot stuck his head in. "I forgot to tell you, I paid ninety-five pounds to Tattersalls on settling up day, last Monday. Will you enter it in my accounts?"

"Certainly," I said, then went on writing. When he left, the door remained open, vexing me slightly, but I did not again look towards the window, where he was still stationed.

When the letters were completed, I gave them to him and looked about for his account book. With only one item to record, I did not bother to remove it, but made the entry in his office. Glancing up, I noticed he was regarding me intently, in a manner that was beginning to set my nerves on edge. I left quickly, before feeling prompted to make a bold comment. I planned to go to see the butler. Philmot asked me, very politely, if I would mind looking over a speech he planned to make in the House. I could hardly refuse, though my opinion would be of little enough use. The subject had to do with the price of corn. As I read, he took up a position behind me to read over my shoulder. I am not an imaginative person. In any case, I was not imagining that Philmot was following me that morning with his eyes, and in many cases his whole body. In a moment, he reached over my shoulder to finger a passage for careful scrutiny; when he lifted his hand from the page, he placed it in a careless way on my shoulder. It felt like a hot iron, so conscious was I of his touch. I pretended to notice nothing amiss in this behavior, but in fact was astonished.

This was not the brash, disrespectful sort of freedom indulged in on that other infamous occasion. It was tentative, hesitant, waiting on his part to see my reaction. He could not know the words jumped in a senseless way before my eyes, with nothing registering on my brain, could not hear the wild beating that was going on inside my breast. After a breathless while I turned to face him. He looked at me a long minute, into my eyes. We seemed transfixed.

"That—that's very interesting. I could hardly understand more than a half of it," I lied.

"Thank you. I consider that high praise, Olivia," he said, and took the speech back. It was the first time he had called me by my Christian name, except for that one occasion I preferred to forget. "Are you free now for our drive?"

"I was going to oversee a few details for your party. My employer, you must know, is so clutch-fisted he has saddled me with a dozen odds and ends, in case I should ever find a moment free of writing."

"I would not want your house management classes to have been in vain. Did you learn anything from my sister's housekeeper, by the by?"

"I hope you will not be disappointed in the way I have arranged things."

"Oh no, I have gotten over my fit of being disappointed in you. Come and show me what you have done."

He held the door, then came with me to view the saloon. "You will see I have saved you a few guineas by removing your palm trees to the corners, thus cutting down on the baskets of flowers."

"Harding never thought of that stunt," he congratulated me. "What are we to eat? If you have not ordered my favorite petits fours from Gunter, I shall either cry or beat you."

"I never thought you would have a sweet tooth!" I was surprised into saying.

"You are judging by my astringent taste in females, I collect? If you are trying to please me, which of course I do not believe for a moment, you will find me not averse to a little sweetness, to lighten the vinegar."

"I did not order any vinegar, Philmot."

"The question is, did you order the petits fours?"

"Four dozen. It is the quantity Harding ordered last time for a party of similar size, so I made sure it was the optimum quantity."

"Poor Harding. I have made you despise the man, sight unseen, and he is really an excellent fellow. That's what happens when we praise someone too much to a person who does not know him. Or *her*. You know, I think, which *her* I am referring to. I daresay if you ever met him, you would be looking as hard as you could for a flaw."

"I would not find one, to judge by what you have told me."

"You can always find one, if you look hard enough. No one is perfect, not even the clever Miss Fenwick, despite the rumors that preceded her arrival."

"It is well you had Lord Strathacona's opinion of me to balance the scale. I would given an ear to know what he said."

"It don't bear repeating," he replied, in a teasing way. "All true too. Well, perhaps I would not agree you are *the most managing female ever born,* but then Strathacona never met my Great Aunt Matilda. Aunt Marion's mama, if you are unaware of it. The daughter's managing capabilities have fallen off since her brain is rotted with trying to learn French. She used to take better care of me."

"Why do you have her live with you, if you dislike managing women?"

"Oh I did not say anything about disliking them. It is Strathacona who mentions his abhorrence of the breed every two minutes. Between the two of us, I think he and Deb could use a manager."

"If that is a hint I should apply for the job . . . ."

"You already have a job. And do it very well too, to my infinite chagrin. I had hoped you would not, you see, so I would be justified in all the trouble I have caused you. This tangled conversation is in the nature of an apology, Olivia, in case even *your* superior abilities fail to recognize it for one."

As his treatment of me had been harsh, I did not bother with the insincerity of asking what he apologized for. "I made my share of errors," I admitted, with a memory of having left Dottie untended at the modiste's shop.

Philmot remained home to luncheon on that day, after which we went for our drive. I was not displeased when it was his open curricle that was drawn up in front of the house, not displeased either when our route was to the busiest section of town, Hyde Park, where we were seen by all the ton, I sitting next Lord Philmot in his carriage. We stopped at the barrier, where I was introduced to several eminent persons as "my house guest, Miss Fenwick," with never a word about secretaries, governesses or anything else.

"You are a friend of Lady Beaton, are you not?" one gentleman asked me. "I think I have seen you driving her carriage."

"Not really," I began to explain, but was quickly outspoken by Philmot.

"You are mistaken, John," he said abruptly, then began to talk about some other matter.

As we drove on, he said, "I made an error in leading you to buy Lady Beaton's tilbury. My groom has been taking a close look at it, and has discovered the wheels to be badly skewed."

"It runs quite smoothly."

"It could be dangerous. You must not drive it till he has got it fixed. You will dislike being without it, but must feel free to borrow something of mine till it is repaired. Something other than this curricle and greys, that is to say," he added. He was out of reason proud of his unmanageable team of goers.

"How long will it take?" I asked, sorry to be losing my tilbury just when it seemed I was to gain a little free time.

"Not long. I'll let you know when it is ready. Meanwhile use my chaise. I don't use it in good weather."

I had not the least objection to being carried about the city in Philmot's crested carriage, and spent the next moments trying to think of some destination worthy of it.

I knew from handling his correspondence that Philmot was promised to a ball that evening, and thought I would be dining with Miss Millichope alone again, sharing an evening by the cold grate. With this idea in my head, I made no elegant toilette, but came to the saloon before dinner in my simplest gown, a bronze sarcenet. Miss Millichope was with her nephew when I came down. "This is a surprise, Philmot," she said. Then she smiled at me, and went on, "Perhaps Miss Fenwick would like to come with us. She likes music."

"I am accompanying my aunt to a musical evening at a friend's home after dinner," he explained. "An Italian tenor and a string quartet. Does Miss Fenwick like music enough to endure such an outing?" he asked, smiling. "Lady Varley is having the do. I know little of her taste in music, but can vouch for the quality of her spouse's cellar. If it gets too rough, we can always sneak away to a parlor and drink."

"Are you not going to the ball?"

"Ball?" he asked. "Oh, you refer to Elgin's do. No, the fact is, this liver is still acting up after its torture at Jackson's hands. I am fit for nothing but a quiet evening sitting down, and have offered to accompany my aunt to hear the tenor. We would be happy if you would come with us."

I was pleased to have been included, but could only wonder he would go out at all if he were feeling unwell. The wounded liver did not interfere with his taking a good dinner. I wondered if it were possible he had changed his plans so that I might be included in the outing. Was it ineligible for him to take me, uninvited, to a ball, whereas the less formal concert could more easily accommodate the uninvited?

"I believe I'll change my gown," I said, after we had eaten.

"You don't have to dress up for this," Miss Millichope told me.

"Just put on your diamond necklace and you'll be the most elegant creature there," Philmot suggested.

Naturally I did not confess my diamonds lay on a shelf in some shabby pawn shop, but some of my consternation was to be read on my face. Philmot's eyes flew to my neck when I descended wearing a string of pearls. Before he could speak, I made a comment, totally irrelevant, to divert him.

The music presented was indifferent at best; the audience was most select. There was hardly an untitled head nodding in the whole chamber, and hardly one other than my own and Philmot's that was neither bald nor gray.

"You made a poor choice of outing if it was entertainment you were looking for," I told him between numbers. His restlessness and yawns had not escaped my notice.

"Aunt Marion twisted my arm when she learned I meant to stay home," was his answer. I remembered her expressions of surprise, and was not deceived by his words.

I made the acquaintance of several elderly lords and ladies, and had a fifteen minute discussion with a dowager marchioness about her parrot during intermission. It was a fortune teller, so the story went. I also had a glass of orgeat and a biscuit. If Varley kept a good cellar, he also kept a tight one. Not a drop of wine was served. All in all, not a memorable evening.

It was not till we were home and Miss Millichope had yawned her way upstairs that the subject of diamonds arose. "You decided against being the most elegant creature at the party, I notice," he mentioned, in a casual fashion.

"It is vulgar to strive to outshine all others, don't you think?"

"Yes, I do. I notice you have not worn them since coming here. If there is something amiss with them, you must get it repaired before my ball."

"When is this great occasion?"

"In a few weeks. It is traditionally one of the last of the Season, in early June."

Some quick calculations told me my second quarter salary would not be due so soon. I had spent virtually nothing since coming to him, and was toying with the idea of emptying my purse to get them back. He regarded me closely as this scheme ran through my head. "What have you done with them?" he asked bluntly.

It was no secret that half the aristocracy were in financial trouble from time to time. Harmsworth had laughed and joked about my predicament and his own. This being the case, I answered lightly, "Hawked them. I only got thirty guineas, the piker."

He rolled up his eyes and said a word he ought not to have used in a lady's presence. "I thought you were *sensible!*"

"So I am. I know how to get hold of cash when I am in the basket."

"How could you possibly need money? My sister paid you one hundred guineas two months ago. You don't go anywhere. What foolishness have you been indulging in?"

"Having a foolish and quite unnecessary accident with my carriage. Buying stockings and muslin and gloves. Oh and a bottle of Gowland's lotion for this demanding face of mine. My folly knows no bounds."

"Where did you hawk it?"

"Squibbs was the name of the place."

"That joint! You didn't go there alone I hope."

"I did not go at all. A friend did the deed for me."

"A *gentleman* friend?"

"Oh yes. I could not like to ask a lady to do anything so untoward."

"I did not realize you had a beau," he said, with a certain stiffening of the shoulders that indicated the subject was drawing to a swift close. "This must be a very good friend, to be in on your most intimate secrets."

"A good friend, yes."

"One can only wonder he did not advance you the sum himself, if that is the case."

"Like my profligate self, he was in the basket, or he would likely have made the offer."

"That surprises me. I thought the clever Miss Fenwick would have the foresight to land herself a friend of better fortune."

"I have not found wealthy people to be particularly open-handed," I answered, with a thought of his nip-cheese sister.

He studied me a moment, looking for a personal reference in the remark I expect. Then he shrugged his shoulders, mentioned his fatigue, and said goodnight. It was an entirely unhappy ending to a not very enjoyable evening.

Chapter Seventeen

THE MORNING WAS NO better. Any friendliness that had been developing between us was ended. He came late to his office, mumbled "Good morning," and accepted the opened mail. Half an hour later, he laid it on my desk, the required replies penciled in. He said he had to go out, and left at once. At lunch time, he was still out, though of course he was home in time to make a fresh toilette for his party. My own chief interest in the affair was to see if Harmsworth attended, that I might ask him to redeem my diamonds for me. He would think me a great fool, but I wanted them back.

The throng soon trooping through the portals were

younger and more lively than the ancients met at Lady Varley's musical party. They were, I soon learned, the very pink of the ton. There was hardly a name heard that was not often encountered in the newspaper, and not only in the society columns either. Stars of the Government, business, arts and letters were there. Everyone was there except Lord Harmsworth. Lady Synge and Alice attended, and spent some moments talking to me. Jack and Debbie were there and condescended to inquire how I did. I inquired for the state of the mother-to-be and was told she felt perfectly horrid. And the doctor had forbidden her to ride! He might as well have forbidden her to draw breath. She looked perfectly wretched, all washed out, and with great circles under her eyes. She was not taking proper care of her health. Looking at her from across the room, I felt some pangs of concern, and went to them to urge a proper diet and exercise, for the baby's sake if not her own. They were not at all grateful but said in the snippiest way imaginable that they planned to engage Doctor Croft, and if he was good enough for Princess Charlotte, they did not feel the need of Doctor Fenwick's concern.

"If he is to assist Princess Charlotte, you may be sure he will go to Claremont to reside with her. He won't be much good to you, living outside of London."

They looked stunned when I pointed this rather obvious fact out to them. Soon they were wearing a different expression. Shock, I think, is the best word to describe it. Following the line of their gaze, I noticed that Lady Beaton had decided to discommode Philmot with her presence, uninvited, unless she had wangled an invitation from him. As I was so very vexed with my employer, I was happy to see she had come.

"Lady Beaton!" I exclaimed, smiling a welcome towards the doorway.

"How did *you* find out about her?" Jack asked, staring.

"She was here at the house earlier this week. What is amiss with her, that Philmot is so eager for her absence? I think she is beautiful."

"Good lord!" was his answer. He and Debbie exchanged a look, then Jack dashed across the room to greet her. I looked after him, noticing the lady was causing quite a stir. She was even more gorgeous than the other time. She wore a turban again. Her pelisse had been removed to reveal a perfectly stunning rose colored gown, somewhat more elaborate than any other lady in the saloon wore. Many heads turned to stare, then the level of noise suddenly rose several notches. I looked about to see how Philmot was taking her arrival. He looked once, one short, sharp, angry glare at her, then pointedly turned his back and resumed conversation with another party. It was clear to me, and no doubt to the others, that Jack was trying to guide the lady from the room. His hand was on her arm, his direction towards the archway by which she had entered. She was having none of it. She fought free of Jack's restraining hands, looking around the room for Philmot. I saw her look at his back, with a mischievous sparkle in her eyes. I made sure she was going to approach him, but she continued glancing around, neither speaking nor nodding to anyone till she spotted me.

"Miss Fenwick, so nice to see you again," she called in a good, loud voice, then she began working towards me. The throng fell away to allow her easy passage, while I looked, too surprised to speak. Why should she select *me*, whom she had met exactly once, as her especial friend?

Before she reached me, Philmot was at her elbow. I did not see his approach, for I had my eyes riveted on Lady Beaton. "Kate—so glad you could come," Philmot said, smiling and trying to sound normal, but there was a touch of steel in his eyes. His fingers closed around her elbow in a grip that caused her to wince. I thought she looked frightened, though he could hardly harm her in the middle of his saloon. Without looking at or speaking to any of the hundred guests present, he led her to the edge of the room, talking in a quiet way all the while. Like everyone else present, I followed them with my eyes, noting that before two minutes were up, he was piloting her out the door. When they were gone, the hubbub of raised voices resumed, or increased, for it had not quite stopped.

Such tatters of conversation as "the gall of the creature!" and "Philmot will kill her" were heard to reverberate around the saloon, in outraged accents. Hoping for enlightenment, I wended my way towards Lady Synge. "Shocking performance!" she said. "But Philmot will wrap it up in clean linen. He is good at that. I did not know *you* were acquainted with her, Miss Fenwick."

"Who is she?" I asked, with a premonition that folks would not speak so hard against any lady of propriety.

"Why she is his mistress, Miss Fenwick. That is why he is so angry at her coming here to his home, to meet his friends. A gentleman does not invite his mistress to such a respectable do as this."

"Oh," I said, in a voice so weak I hardly heard it.

"If she thinks to force his hand to marriage with this stunt, she is out in her reckoning. It will turn him against her. Mark my words."

Such a jumbled confusion of thoughts were in my head, I barely heard her. I felt as though I had sustained a severe blow to the stomach. Noticing Lady Synge regarding me strangely, I excused myself and fled the room, at too hot a pace to avoid notice and gossip. I stumbled along the hallway, seeking privacy at the first closed doorway. I wrenched the door open and stopped dead. There in the middle of the room stood the pair of them, locked in a passionate embrace. Alerted by the opening door, they looked up to stare at me. Lady Beaton tossed her head and smiled in triumph. "We have company, darling," she said to him, and laughed, a throaty, delighted gurgle.

Philmot just looked. He dropped his arms, his lower jaw and stood stock still for a moment. There is no describing his expression in one word. He was angry, proud, determined, most nonplussed, but certainly he was not unmoved.

I said, "Excuse me," in a very low voice, and turned to continue my flight. Philmot's office door stood ajar across the hallway. I pelted in and closed the door after me, leaning against it, for I knew my legs would not hold me up unaided. The chair was too far away to tackle it yet. I felt betrayed, as a wife must feel when first she learns of a husband's straying. I don't remember walking to the chair, but I must have. I sat in it a moment later when Philmot came in. I arose immediately, with the absurd thought that he had caught me out, sitting at his desk, where I did not belong.

He looked sheepish, no more. He had recovered his composure more quickly than I. "I came here to get my cheque book, but as you are here, perhaps you'll do it for me. I want a cheque made out for Lady Beaton in the sum of one thousand pounds." He looked a bold challenge at me as he made this speech.

"The job of mistress pays well. Much better than secretary."

"You made it perfectly clear *you* were not interested in the job the first day you were here."

"Yes, for the duties struck me as singularly unpleasant."

"I am getting rid of Kate. That's why the sum is larger than usual."

"Are you indeed? I assume you are parting on the best of terms, to judge by what I have just been subjected to."

"No point aggravating her with half of London in the next room with its ears flapping. She came here to make mischief. She knew it was over between us, and had nothing to lose."

"A good sum to gain, in fact."

"Yes. Will you write up the cheque, please?"

"Do it yourself," I said, and flounced from the room, to go upstairs, for I could not face the guests so soon.

There was no escaping the pair so easily. They were inside my head, her beautiful, taunting, triumphant face, and his arrogant mask, ordering me to write her a cheque. I would have remained forever in my room, had I not been prodded back downstairs by the necessity of seeing Harmsworth. I hoped he might have arrived by that time, for he had received an invitation, despite Philmot's professed dislike of the man. I was forming the idea I would return home to Bath immediately. Lady Synge would not be sorry to be free of me, so there was no compulsion to fill my contract. I would have packed up and left that moment had it not been for my diamonds. I could not go home without them. In my disordered state, it did not occur to me that getting the diamonds would mean emptying my purse, but some trifling pieces of jewelry could have been sacrificed to bring me a few guineas traveling money. Harmsworth must get them back for me, the diamonds. It took me half an hour to screw up my courage to go below, and when at last I went, he was not there. How could I go alone to Squibbs, a disreputable hole in the wall, a haunt of raffish men?

I felt rather than saw Philmot approach from across the room. "Headache all better?" he asked when he was at my side. With so many ears on the stretch, I was not about to enter into an argument.

"I am looking for Lord Harmsworth. Do you know if he is here?"

"He's gone to the race meet. He has a filly running in the Oaks at Epsom. Why do you want to see that rattle?"

"It is a personal matter."

"You had better unthaw your face if you don't want every gossip in the room talking about you," was his next speech, delivered in a curt tone.

"They have a more interesting tidbit to discuss today, if I am not mistaken."

"I am sorry you were involved in the disreputable affair."

"I was not involved, Lord Philmot. If your mistress decided to pay you a call at an inopportune moment, it has nothing to do with me."

"You are, unfortunately, mistaken on that score. It will soon blow over if we keep our heads." As he spoke, he led me to a small group of his friends who were discussing some new dramatic wonder at Covent Garden. "We haven't seen that one yet," he told them, his glance identifying myself as the other part of the "we." "Olivia might like it. She enjoyed *The Provok'd Wife* which we saw earlier this season."

I could not imagine why he was at such rounds to make me seem a closer friend than I was. There was more of this intimate chatter, during which I don't think I said more than two words.

"Your cousins are preparing to leave," he said later, still in front of friends. "We must say goodbye to Deb and Jack." This too struck me as an unnecessary trotting out of my relationship to the Strathaconas.

"Why are you trying to make me sound respectable?" I asked when we had got away.

"Aren't you?" was the only answer I had.

Deb was not feeling well, which accounted for her leaving early. The others stayed on for another interminable hour. This party, so looked forward to, was a disaster for me. When the last guest had straggled to the door, we stood alone in the rubble of empty glasses, discarded serviettes and partially empty plates. "Thank God that's over!" he said, snatching the words from my mouth.

"An unfortunate affair," I agreed drily.

"You are returning to Russell Square today," he informed me.

"I cannot go yet. Dottie . . ."

"The period of contagion is over. You are leaving within the hour."

"Why? What will you do for a secretary?" I asked this, not from any desire to remain, but because I feared for my reception at Synges.

"I can write my own letters. Get your things together now. We'll leave in one hour."

"I'll take my own carriage."

"You are not to be seen in that rig. I told you it is unsafe. I'll send it over when it is repaired."

I was too surprised, too utterly confused to argue. "Very well."

As I readied my belongings to leave, I was not unaware of the injustice of it all. Philmot's mistress had misbehaved, and was rewarded with one thousand pounds. I, perfectly innocent, was rewarded by the loss of my position.

Chapter Eighteen

I DON'T SUPPOSE MORE than three words were exchanged en route from Philmot's place to Russell Square. It was not till we were at the front door that Philmot said, "This will blow over in no time."

"I have not done anything wrong," I pointed out.

"Appearances can be misleading."

"It would take an active imagination to read a brief visit, chaperoned the whole time by your aunt, into a scandal."

"There is no shortage of active imaginations in London," he replied. "Then too there is your reputation as an—*unconventional* lady."

His sister was waiting for us. She was on guard at the door of her saloon to catch us as we entered. Whether she had set Dottie at the door of the smaller parlor on the other side of the hallway I do not know, but I would not put it past her. Dottie, fairly well recovered from her spots but still pale, beckoned me into the smaller parlor.

"You go along and speak to Dottie," Lady Synge said

in a kindly way. "Philmot and I will decide what is best to be done."

It is indefensible to pick the brains of a mere child, so I shall not bother to defend my action in questioning Dottie to learn what was afoot. In any case, she was agog to tell me all. "Isn't it exciting, Miss Fenwick?" she exclaimed, as soon as I had inquired of her health. I knew it was not the chicken pox of which she spoke.

"It is a great to-do about nothing, if you want my opinion," I said.

"Nothing? How can you say so?" Her brown puppy eyes held a trace of pity, that emotion so unappetizing to the recipient. I would rather be hated than pitied. "Mama says it is all Uncle Phil's fault in having you stay with him," she rattled on. You may be sure I did not try to stop her. "And of course his having got Lady Beaton's carriage for you in the first place, for it looks as though he was setting *you* up as his mistress, giving you the same carriage. That is what has got Lady Beaton jealous as a green cow, Mama says. As though Uncle Phil would have his *mistress* stay at his own home. *I* think it more likely Lady Beaton was afraid he meant to marry you, and that is why she flew into the boughs. Is she terribly beautiful, Miss Fenwick?"

"Yes, very," I said, while my head grappled with all the implications of her remarks.

"I wonder how much money he gives her. She is shockingly expensive, you must know."

"Did your mother speak to you of all this, Dottie?" I asked, to be sure it was not just imaginings on the child's part.

"Oh, no! Pray do not tell her I know. I listened when she talked it over with Papa after the party. *He* says he will not have you back in his house, but you must not worry about him. Mama says he must, or your reputation will be ruined, and she won't have it said she hired a lightskirt to teach her children. Besides, Philmot told Mama they must take you, and he can always talk them around. He said he has been at pains for a few days now to show the world you are not only respectable but above reproach. He expected trouble when Lady Beaton came right to his house. She sounds a brazen hussy."

I sat, stunned into silence, considering the recent past in the light of her revelations. The public drive in the park, the invitation to Lady Varley's musical evening, the intimate talk before his friends at his own party—all done to set my name well apart from the lightskirts of the world, where it would never have been had he not encouraged me to buy his mistress's tilbury. He had never cared a jot for me, but was only doing his gentlemanly duty to protect my name. Raised voices issued from behind the closed door of the saloon, with no words being intelligible. I sat listening, enjoying all the vivid discomfort of being unwanted in any of their houses. I was nothing but a nuisance to them, and an expensive nuisance at that.

Without giving the matter rational consideration, I determined I would not be billeted on any unwilling family. I would climb into my harlot's carriage and go home to Bath. Oh, but first I must get my diamonds. Just before I despaired, it popped into my head that I had relatives in the city with whom I was on terms. I could go to the Danners, Papa's relatives in Hans Town, stay with them a few days, till I could get to Squibbs. Indeed, the captain might very well be the means of retrieving my necklace. Oh but I would hate to ask him, such an oldfashioned, respectable man.

Dottie chattered on, very excitedly, while I did this mental figuring. When the door of the saloon opened, I had my speech ready. It was a triumphant Lady Synge who issued from the door. She had coerced the ostrich into accepting my presence, then.

"My dear Miss Fenwick," she began, trying to smile a welcome.

"Lady Synge, before you say a word, you must allow me to speak." I jumped in. Philmot looked wary, but I caught only a glimpse from the corner of my eye, for I did not deign to look right at him. "This predicament Philmot has landed me in by foisting his mistress's old carriage off on to me is very vexing, is it not? I think the best thing for me to do is go to my relatives in town for the remainder of the season."

"Excellent!" the ostrich squawked.

"Elderly cousins who live quietly at the edge of town," I informed her, watching with amusement while a smile lit her face. "They will not have heard any disturbing rumors about me, or realize the infamy of my chariot," I added with a certain relish.

"Couldn't be better," Synge said. "It is all settled."

"No, it will be better if she stays here," Philmot disagreed.

"Naturally your sister would not want it said a female of low morals had been instructing her children," I said knowingly, "but it will perhaps be remembered as well that my father is the Dean of Bath, while the cousins to whom I go are also utterly respectable. As I have actually done nothing wrong except heed bad advice, let us hope the gossip will settle where it belongs, and not on me."

"There is certainly something in that," Synge pointed out to his recalcitrant relatives.

"Is there any trusting Kate Beaton to hold her tongue, and not pretend she is Miss Fenwick's bosom bow, as she was certainly trying to let on at your party?" Lady Synge asked her brother.

"If she is recalcitrant, Philmot can always give her another cheque," I suggested.

"Phil, you greenhead! You didn't give her *more* money!" his sister charged angrily. I glanced for the first time at him. He looked as though he would happily murder his sister. I could not but wonder what sums had been passed prior to the thousand pounds. And he had bypassed my accounting books too, the sly one.

"We'll be lucky to get a commoner for Alice, with all this scandal surrounding the family," Synge declared impatiently. "It is all settled. Miss Fenwick goes to her cousins."

"All settled but for Philmot to send me my tilbury," I agreed.

"You cannot be seen in that rig!" Philmot disagreed, very loudly.

"A pity you had not thought so when you arranged for me to buy it! I cannot afford to squander large sums of money on useless items. I have not so generous a patron as Lady Beaton."

"You must not be angry at Philmot," Lady Synge began in a conciliating way. "There would have been no harm in your having the carriage when you were working for *me,* Miss Fenwick. None of us thought, when you went to Philmot, how it would look. But now with Kate barging in at the party showing everyone she was jealous . . . well, you see how it looks. Folks will take the notion you have replaced her."

"They will not think anything of the sort," Philmot insisted.

"Why do you not want me seen in the carriage then?" I asked.

He was stymied, for of course he knew perfectly well his sister was right. My reputation was so ruined I did not see how it could ever be repaired. Strangely enough,

187

I did not care much. Of greater importance to me was to get away. "You will send my carriage right over, please," I said, directing a command to Philmot.

"Very well, but I trust you will have the wisdom not to be seen in town in it."

"You will find me more discreet than Lady Beaton," I assured him. "I do not relish having it said I was ever your mistress. Good day." I turned and walked, stiff as a poker, up to my old room. Once there, I could not think why I had bothered to climb the stairs. Nothing of mine remained but the memories. I had once actually been happy in this room. Happy and naïve, to think a lady of no importance could palm herself off as anything but a governess. I would have fared better had I behaved as what I was, hired help. I could not afford this double life. I had lost not only my diamonds, but quite possibly my reputation as well.

Later, Lady Synge came up to tell me Philmot had left, and would send my carriage right over. "You cannot be thinking of landing in on your cousins unannounced at night," she pointed out. "Write them a note, and go in the morning, Miss Fenwick. Stay here tonight. No one will know you are here." I expect that last sentence was one she had said to her husband, and repeated unthinkingly to me.

It told me how low I had sunk. I wrote to the Danners, who had the human charity to reply in the affirmative, and the grace to do it that same night, with enthusiasm. I remained in my room all night. Alice was at a rout, but Dottie bore me company for an hour, during which I urged her to continue her studies when she felt more stout. She wanted to come and see me, but I discouraged this, saying I would not be there long, and she could not go out yet.

I left early in the morning, never bothered to unpack my bags at all. They were sent over the night before, and taken to Danners in Synge's carriage. I prevaricated a little in my story to them. I said Miss Dorothy had the chicken pox, but did not tell them when she had contracted the disease. I did not wish to scandalize them with the whole truth.

Chapter Nineteen

LIFE IN HANS TOWN was very different from life in the west end of London. It was much better. I made myself useful around the house, for they had three children and little hired help. I also took Mrs. Danner for local rides in my infamous carriage. In the evenings, I read stories to the children, played cards with the parents after the youngsters were tucked into bed, and enjoyed such provincial company as came to call.

"Miss Fenwick has been staying with the aristocracy," Mrs. Danner announced to the first set of callers.

"A governess for the Synges," I said quickly.

"Olivia, I am sure a governess does not go to plays and parties," she laughed.

"They were lenient," I agreed. "Most governesses are not so fortunate, but I was employed by the Synge family, not a house guest."

"Miss Fenwick is related to the Monternes—a marchioness is her cousin," was the next proud boast. "She has stayed with them too."

"Only second cousins to my mama," I said scrupulously, remarking how the connection impressed these simple folk. Just as it had impressed me in the old days, when I thought a title conferred some extraordinary qualities of chivalry, or worth. I knew better now. They were no better than the rest of us. Some of them were a good deal worse, as they came heavily encumbered with pride. They also had money, which allowed them to indulge their every whim.

I found I could not tell the Danners how foolish I had been, and therefore could not seek their help in retrieving my necklace. They were too decent—would be shocked at my dreadful carrying on. My salvation came in the form of a new acquaintance. A Mr. Teasdale called on my cousins, and the next day came to call on me, to ask me to a lecture that evening. I presumed most outrageously on his good nature to ask him to take my thirty pounds and go to Squibbs. When he came back, he still carried the pawn ticket and the money.

"There was some error. This pawn ticket is for a watch fob. A little golden shell with a pearl in it."

That particular watch fob was known to me. It belonged to Harmsworth. A week or two ago, I would have assumed it to have been an honest error. With the scales removed from my eyes, I thought it more likely Harmsworth had pulled this stunt purposely. It hardly seemed worth while trying to be in touch with him. I was sure he had sold my diamonds, pocketing the bulk of the money himself. Yes, how had he afforded a horse running in the Oaks, when he was as broke as I? It was possible he thought to repay me with his winnings, *if* he won. As the matter was of such importance to me, I once again imposed on my new acquaintance to take a note to Harmsworth asking about the ticket. He came back to tell me Lord Harmsworth was out of town, adding that this might be a ruse on his lordship's part, as there were bailiffs in the house looking for him. Obviously his horse had not come in first.

There was really no excuse to remain in London. I wrote Harmsworth a letter requesting him to write to me at Bath when he returned, on the off chance I might yet get my necklace back. Hints about reporting the matter to Bow Street were added to encourage him to act properly in the matter, though I doubted very much he could get them back if he wanted to. It weighed heavy on my heart that I had urged Alice to marry this scoundrel, but at least she had not followed my bad advice. Planning to leave the next day, I also dropped a note of farewell to Lady Synge and the Strathaconas. I purposely withheld my address. I was in no mood to receive either of them, should they, by some odd chance, take into their heads to bid me a personal farewell. The arrangement for my transport, as I could not go alone, was for the eldest daughter to accompany me home, with her return to her parents to be arranged by my father. There were frequently friends of ours coming up to London, who could see her home.

I put the whole thing from my mind the minute the notes were posted. My opinion of my old aristocratic companions was so low I hesitated before even bothering to write. As a farewell gesture, I took the two younger girls out for a spin in my tilbury that last afternoon. Their little noses were sadly out of joint that they were not going to Bath with me. It was a beautiful day, with summer practically upon us. We stayed out later than we should have done, rushing home close to five for dinner. They kept country hours at the Danners. The

191

girls clung to my hands when I entered the house, all of us chattering and laughing.

"Lettie, we're home!" I called, and strode into her parlor, to see Lord Philmot comfortably ensconced in a chair, holding a tea cup in his hand. He was conversing with Mrs. Danner, seeming very much at home.

"Olivia, nice to see you," he said, rising up to make his bow. "We had your note. I have just been telling Mrs. Danner how remiss you were in not having given us your address here. I have been not less than three times to Hans Town trying to find you. One might even be forgiven for thinking she did not wish to see us," he added in a jocular way to his hostess, who laughed merrily.

"That is not like Olivia, to forget anything," she said.

"Hello, Philmot. It was not necessary for you to come in person to pay your adieux."

"Very true, but my letter was not clever enough to find its way without me."

I presented the girls to him before sitting down. I was determined to be no more than coolly polite, and would have been less than that had it not been for Mrs. Danner's presence. I enquired for the Synges, particularly Dottie. I was told she was hale and hearty and as ill-mannered as ever. Debbie was complaining of nausea. Jack was taking her home to Dawlish. "They will be away for my ball," he added. "I have your invitation here, by the by." He extracted a white square and handed it to me.

I did not bother to take it. "I am leaving tomorrow, Philmot," I told him, stiff as starch.

"My ball is tonight, Ma'am," he replied, with a triumphant smile. "Fairly well snatched your excuse away, did I not? Tell her she must go, Mrs. Danner."

Mrs. Danner sat regarding us in some confusion. She apparently found it odd I had never so much as mentioned Lord Philmot's name once in all the days I had been with them. "That sounds lovely, Olivia," she said, smiling at my good fortune in rounding off my visit in this high fashion.

"We plan to leave early in the morning. We can make it with only one night at an inn if we do."

"It seems a shame to miss the ball," she went on, with a look of planning to push me into acceptance.

"I packed my trunks this afternoon. My gowns would be a mass of wrinkles."

"There's plenty of time to press one."

"No really, I do not wish to attend. Thank you very much, Philmot."

Mrs. Danner was fairly astute, but had she been as dull as tarnished silver she would have realized Philmot wished for privacy. He glanced first at me, with impatience and suppressed passion (angry, you understand), then at herself and the girls, in the way of one who is restraining himself because of the company. The signs were unmistakable.

"Time to get you two cleaned up for dinner," Mrs. Danner said, arising and taking each girl by one hand to drag them unwillingly from the room.

She could not have been a yard from the doorway before he broke into a very different sort of speech from that he had been using. "I suppose this is your idea of a clever trick, hiding yourself out here and telling no one where you are. Have you any idea the shifts I have been put to to find you? I hired the Bow Street Runners!"

"You didn't!" I gasped.

"Yes, in desperation I did after I learned you had not sneaked off home to Bath, as I first suspected you meant to do."

"You mean you have written to my father! How *dare* you! He will be worried sick."

193

"You mean you haven't let him know you're here?"

"I wrote a day ago to tell him I was coming home. He will have received it by now I hope. When did you . . ."

"Two days after you left. Before I called in Bow Street."

"You incorrigible busybody! What business is it of *yours* where I go?"

"It is because of me you are in this fix. You made *that* perfectly clear before you left us."

"I am not in a fix. If the ton wish to have a few titters because they think you took on a new flirt before dumping the old, it is nothing to me."

"*After* dumping the old. I had already rid myself of Kate Beaton before you came to me."

"You gave her money long after I was there."

"*You're* the one gave her cash from my strong box!"

"And how dare you include my name in the same breath as that woman anyway!"

"That was a misunderstanding. Kate would not have come landing in on us if she had still been under my protection. She knew she had nothing to lose. . . ."

"A great deal to gain. A thousand pounds, was it not?"

"I had already paid her. Unbeknownst to me she had another lot of bills unpaid. She threatened to go into the saloon and make a scene."

"You were kissing her. No doubt she forced *that* on you too."

"Kissing her goodbye. At the time, nothing and no price seemed too high to pay to be rid of her once for all."

"You can get her back now, if you haven't already. Just as well you parted on such amicable terms."

"Look," he said, splaying out his hands. "I know it is all my fault you were put in an untenable position. It was unfortunate, the business of my having got her tilbury for you. Lady Synge explained that to you. After all the fuss, however, you can imagine what people think. You were seen driving her carriage, you were seen in my company. Kate comes storming into the party and singles you out for attention. You were already known as a very *modern* thinker. The Fowlers delighted in spreading their story. The conclusion is nearly inevitable. Folks think you are my mistress. I have come to make reparation. Your only salvation is marriage. I am going to marry you."

"Are you indeed? How very *charitable* of you, but I would prefer to remain ruined, thank you very much."

"Don't be so stubborn, Olivia. You only came to London to make a match. Oh I know you claimed an interest in education, but it was no more than a ruse to rub shoulders with the ton. You have overestimated the worth of a title, but I don't think it necessary to tell you that rather obvious fact."

"I did not come to London to meet the aristocracy! You forget I stayed with the Monternes a year before coming here. I met a dozen dukes and duchesses."

"God yes, and never talked about anything else but the Tavistocks and Monternes, till we were all sick to death of hearing about them. The Monternes *used* you, and then laughed at you behind your back. Debbie at least . . . If you were not so blinded by this infatuation for titles you would see it. Has she ever *once* been to Russell Square to call on you?"

"No, you will be delighted to hear she has not!"

"I am not delighted. I think it damned impertinent of her. Ill-bred, equine behavior, as one would suspect of Strathacona's lady. I expect she will give birth to a foal when her time is due."

"That's a fine way to talk about your friends."

"Friends? I wouldn't have given them the time of day if it were not for curiosity to hear what they had to say of *you*. They were the only ones in town who actually knew anything about you. Till I realized they were a pair of yahoos themselves, I put too much credit in their opinion. But I had eyes to see they were correct in thinking you lusted after titles and ton. Even toadying up to that jackanapes of a Harmsworth."

"I don't know who you think you are, talking to me like that."

"I am a *Lord*, Olivia. A genuine peer of the realm. What other qualification should I require?"

"A little common decency would not go amiss. And don't think I would ever have gone to your home had I had the least idea what you are really like. I regret I ever locked horns with you."

"Sorry your halo ever became entangled in my horns you mean. Don't think I would have asked you had I realized you were not free to leave at your own pleasure. How was I to suspect you worked from necessity when you put up at the Pulteney, wore diamonds, and had set up your own carriage? I took you for an extremely eccentric lady but definitely one of independent means. Till I learned you had hawked your diamonds, I had no notion you were not."

"I don't see what all this has to do with anything."

"To err is human, you said. To blame it on someone else is also human. I am trying to allot the correct share of blame to each. *I* acted badly because *you* misled me as to your true circumstances. I would not have behaved as I did to an ordinary governess, one who was dependent on her position."

"I expect you would not have given the world the idea she was in a bracket with Lady Beaton either."

"I came here to rectify that unfortunate business. I am going to marry you."

"I wouldn't have you if you were the King of England."

"A *sincere* refusal would give me a better opinion of

you. I shall be back tomorrow with a ring and license."

"I won't be here."

"I think you will, *Lady* Philmot."

"I would sooner die an old maid in Bedlam or Newgate than accept your impertinent, condescending *insult* of an offer. Whatever my *former* opinion of the aristocracy may have been, and I admit it was higher than justified, you may be sure I have rectified it. I have learned something from my experience at your hands." I made a curtsey and turned to leave.

"What about my ball? I told everyone you would be there."

"You will have to tell them you were mistaken," I replied, and swept out the door.

Hearing his footfalls coming behind me, I hastened to the stairway and got halfway up it before he called after me. I did not stop, but went to my room to consider in peace and quiet this extraordinary visit. What a degrading proposal of marriage, and to be told into the bargain his opinion of me would be higher if I refused! My opinion of him would not be quite so low had he not bothered to make it, and I wished I had thought to tell him so.

Chapter Twenty

THE BOLT OF INDIAN muslin returned to Bath with
the starch out of it, its blooms sadly faded, a rent here
and there in the fabric, but with still a few years' wear
left in it. My father was happy to see me, Doris somewhat less so I think, though she was polite. "I never
could see how it would work out," she admitted. "Neither fish nor fowl, being a grand lady with a carriage
and diamonds, and working as a governess. That is not
the carriage Mrs. Crewes described to us, is it, Olivia?"
You will notice I had finally become Olivia, at my own
request.

"No, I traded it on a new one."

"I made sure you would be wearing your diamonds,
your first night home, and with company for dinner,"
Papa added. He had invited neighbors in, but they had
left early.

"The clasp is loose, Papa. I must have it repaired
before I wear them again." Lying to my own father and
stepmama! I should have confessed the truth, but even

198

after my humiliation in London, some pride remained with me.

"So the young lady caught the chicken pox," Doris said next. "Very kind of the Danners to have you." She smiled at Miss Danner, who sat with us. "Why did you not go back to the Synges when she was cured? You were ten days at Danners. We did not know what to think when Lady Synge's brother wrote for your address. I thought from his letter they expected you back."

"Why Doris, you sound as though you want to be rid of me!"

"I did not mean that. This is your home. You must always be welcome here."

Such unenthusiastic remarks as this showed me how unwelcome I was, but I would show her I had changed. I *would*. During Miss Danner's visit, I was greatly occupied showing her a good time, to repay her parents' kind hospitality to me. After her return had been arranged, I turned my talents to ingratiating myself with Doris. It was pathetically easy, for she was eager for my friendship. We shopped together on Milsom Street. There was some unsuspecting wisdom buried in her ample bosom. She was not fooled into laying out fifteen shillings for Indian muslin. "What a take-in!" she declared. "No more threads to the inch than in the nine shilling. One would have to be a flat to pay more." I was careful not to find her selections garish. Actually she looked well in the more lively shades she favored, and as Papa adored them, why should I tell her they were not worn in London? She would not be adorning Almacks or Carlton House in her green and gold striped gown. She would be sitting in her saloon, or a neighbor's.

I made no demur when she selected those sentimental novels and poems that appealed to her particular nature. Her taste was at least more refined than Miss Millichope's. I urged her to try one of Mrs. Radcliffe's gothic novels, and made a new fan for that genre. She doted on them. As I had some familiarity with them from my greener years, I could point her to the best of them.

"I had no idea you liked this sort of thing, Olivia," she said happily. "I thought they would be too simple for your taste."

"No, I enjoy them very much."

We stitched together on the green and yellow striped silk. "Why do you not try the new slit sleeve, Doris? They are wearing nothing else in London, and you have such pretty arms."

"I would like to, but your Papa would not approve. In his position you know . . ."

"He won't disapprove of anything *you* do."

"He won't *say* anything, but he won't like it. I am a minister's wife now, and must act the part. No point getting above myself." More wisdom, learned too late.

On another occasion she said happily, "I must confess, Olivia, I was worried when I heard you were coming home. I was afraid we should not rub along together, but I see now I worried for nothing. Your Papa always told me we would be friends, but I thought you were too clever and stiff for me."

I was happy to learn I had made myself acceptable, but there was an undeniable lack in my own life. The extreme edges of Doris's and Papa's daring and willingness to dabble in cultural matters just touched that point where mine began. I hope this was not pride leading me astray once again, but while I *do* enjoy an occasional gothic, it is in the nature of a sweet after a more substantial meal. There were no potatoes and meat with Doris's intellectual diet, just the dessert. A few tentative suggestions of essays were politely but firmly rejected.

Lady Monterne wrote from Dawlish, having found a new use for me. She was taking Sylvia for a tour of the lake district for the summer, and wanted me to go to them in September when they returned. "Odd she did not offer to take you with them on the holiday," Doris said, when I showed her the letter. "It sounds a lovely trip. I see she mentions Deborah will be at home for her lying-in, and you could help them out with that."

"Very kind of them," I said in a caustic tone. Deborah had a lot of nerve to suggest anything of the sort after the way she had treated me in London. I wondered if that conversation overheard when I barged in to visit her mother had not been about myself. "Bossy old scold" or something of the sort, she had said. The curt note sent back by me refusing the offer was couched in such terms as made a second request for my services as unpaid governess and nurse unlikely.

I harked back often to my experiences in the city. It seemed as though on every occasion when my path had crossed that of the nobility, I had been used badly. The Synges had all but thrown me into the streets, Harmsworth had stolen my necklace, and Philmot had tried to seduce me. Failing in that, he had done a pretty fair job of ruining my reputation anyway, due to his own amorous intrigue with an expensive trollop. The impudent offer of marriage rankled with all the rest. What a merry chase he would have led me, reminding me with each new affair he undertook that I knew what he was before I married him. I had seen more love, compassion and true happiness at home and at Danners' than in any noble mansion. The only person I missed was Dottie. When I received a letter from her one day, I felt tears stinging my eyes. Wishing privacy to peruse it, I took it to my room.

Dottie had sunk back to her execrable manner of expressing herself, without my stern influence. For half a page, I could not make heads nor tails of it all. Philmot was furious about it; Mama insisted it was a wonderful match; and Alice said she would go through with it, even if she hated him, because she had had a falling out with Captain Tierney. Not till I got to the very bottom of the page did the awful name of Lord Harmsworth pop out and hit me between the eyes. Good God, how was it possible? Alice was promised to Lord Harmsworth, the marriage to take place in two weeks time. The announcements were out, and would I not *please* write to Mama, for she spoke of Miss Fenwick still with admiration, and Dottie felt—how had she discovered it—that I did not like Harmsworth. I must have let something drop during our last conversations, though I could not recall it.

My duty was clear. I must inform the Synges what sort of a man Harmsworth was. One hesitates to put such incriminating matters in black and white, in case the letter should go astray. Or perhaps the tedium of my life was goad enough to make me welcome the excuse to return to London. I felt the affair was partly my fault. I had talked Harmsworth up to Alice, and had never told any of them the truth about him. It was not a fear for the rattle's reputation that had kept my lips sealed either; it was pride. I was not eager to confess to anyone that I had been made a dupe of, but I must tell them now. While the mood of resolution was upon me, I went to Papa and confessed all.

"The bounder! Stole your mama's diamonds!" he exclaimed, pale with shock.

"In a way he did. He said he pawned it for thirty guineas, but the chit did not get it back. For an outright sale he would have gotten more than thirty guineas."

"I paid a hundred for it twenty years ago. It is worth hundreds by now. Why did you not tell me, Olivia?"

"I was ashamed of my folly, and did not want to worry you."

"What else have you not told me, foolish girl? It was not like you to refuse Lady Monterne's invitation to Dawlish. Never mind, I shall learn the truth. I am going to London with you. We shall call Harmsworth to account for this business."

Awful visions of a duel and a dead father reared up in my head. "No, no, I had much better go alone."

"Alone? You have proved to me you are too green to be about the countryside alone. It is my fault for having allowed it. I admit I did not try very hard to keep you home, Livvie, for you and Doris did not hit it off as I hoped you would. I thought you were clever enough to take care of yourself."

"I thought so too. I was mistaken. Come with me then, if you think it for the best, but you must not challenge him to a duel."

"You forget I am a church man. I shall call in Bow Street, and have him clapped in irons if he does not give back the diamonds."

"How sensible you are! Why didn't I do that?"

"Because you are a ninnyhammer, like your mama."

In the end, we took Doris along for the drive. She seldom went to London, and thus greeted it as a great outing. "We'll put up at the Clarendon, and I shall go to see Lady Synge," I outlined as we drove quickly through the green countryside.

"We'll put up at Reddishes for half the price, and *I* shall go to see Lord Synge," Papa contradicted.

"Reddishes is not at all elegant, Papa."

"Good."

"We don't want to be too elegant," Doris pointed out. With a view of her green and yellow striped silk still in

203

my mind, I felt perhaps she was right. My old pride was creeping up on me again. Even—how shameful to confess it—I was wondering what impression Papa would make on the Synges and Lord Philmot. Why was I worrying what a confirmed lecher and a superficial pair of noble nobodies cared about him, who had never harmed a soul in his life, but done a great deal of good. He was worth more than the pack of them rolled up in one. I stayed in our room at the hotel with Doris while papa went to pay the necessary call on Lord Synge, to acquaint him with the character of his proposed son-in-law. There was virtually nothing for me to do. We ordered tea and a newspaper to while away the hour and more we had to wait.

"I haven't been to London in an age. Isn't it exciting?" Doris asked as she poured our tea.

My heart went out to her. Exciting, to be pouring tea in a room no larger than a closet, with a view of another brick wall close enough out the window that one could touch it. "Just being here, I mean," she added, reading the surprise on my face. "My, such crowds in the street. I do wish we could go out a little."

"When Papa gets this business settled, we shall go shopping, and perhaps to a play this evening, if Papa is agreeable," I promised rashly. She beamed like a baby being offered a lollipop.

"I think I'll buy a yard of blond lace to use in the neck of my new gown," she confided, with a daring giggle.

"I know just where to get it," I told her, refraining from mentioning that the neckline was the best part of her new gown, and it would be a pity to conceal it.

The hour came and went. The tea was drunk, the pot grew cold, the newspaper had been perused for interesting items, and still Papa did not return. As the shadows lengthened, I suggested we make our toilette for dinner in the dining room belowstairs.

Doris drew forth from her clothespress not the green and yellow—that she would save for the night at the theater—but an even worse creation in bright blue, with black lace. I was requested to do up her hair, which I did, employing only the beaded combs for ornaments, and laying aside the black ostrich feathers as too handsome for a simple spot like Reddishes. She was disappointed, but ready to take my counsel on sartorial matters. Uncaring for the opinion of provincials, I wore a plain gold crepe gown, with only my pearls for adornment.

"Why Olivia, you dress up better than that at home," she chided.

"My shawl has gold threads, and a three inch fringe," I explained, selecting a fancy shawl to please her.

I looked with silent regret to see it was her white shawl Doris planned to wear, when she had a perfectly good black one that would have subdued her outfit. "How do I look?" she asked, patting her curls.

"Very chic. You will turn all their heads."

The door opened and Papa stepped in at a jaunty pace. "What happened?" we demanded in unison.

"I spoke to Synge. He was not sorry to hear the story, to tell the truth. It seems his daughter only accepted the offer in spite, and has been spouting like a watering pot ever since doing it. They were at their wits' end how to break it off, but this gives them an excellent reason. He sent a note around to Harmsworth not five minutes after my arrival, but there was no answer. The bounder did not dare to show his nose at the door. I cannot imagine how you came to have doings with such a person, Livvie."

"It was worth my necklace if it prevents Alice from

making this dreadful misalliance," I said, much cheered to hear of Synge's rational behavior.

"There was another fellow there, brother to Lady Synge, the one who wrote us at Bath. He seems to think he might get your diamonds back for you," Papa informed me.

"Lord Philmot?" I asked, experiencing a quake inside me.

"Aye, that's the name. He seems a reasonable fellow. He is very generous. He has offered to put us up at his place for a few days, as I mentioned the cost of staying here at Reddishes to chase after Harmsworth."

"No! I would prefer not to, Papa."

"You can talk about it over dinner. The Synges insisted we take our meat with them, to pay us for our trouble in bringing this news. I came to collect you ladies. Give me a minute to change."

"Oh no! We would rather eat here, would we not, Doris?" I implored.

"I was looking forward to a hotel dining room, but a lord's table is even better. You will like it, Olivia. You are always fond of meeting with your high friends."

"No, really! We are very fagged from the trip. I would prefer to stay here." I was suddenly struck with inspiration. *I* would stay behind, and let the others go.

Before I could broach this plan, however, Papa went on with another piece of information that made me less reluctant to go to Russell Square. "I have already accepted, but if you are really knocked up, I'll send a note around to them. Their table will be nearly empty. Philmot could not accept an offer either. He had a party on at his own place, a dinner party, and had to dash off. You can discuss with Lady Synge whether you want to stay with her brother."

"We could leave early," Doris suggested, with a hopeful glance to see if I would not change my mind.

"I would like to see the girls," I said. So long as there was no need to see Philmot, I did not in the least mind seeing the Synges either.

Without further ado, Papa went through the adjoining door to his room to make his toilette. Before long, Doris was called to help him tie his cravat.

The Synges made us welcome very civilly. Lord Synge even took me aside and made a sort of apology for his former brusque treatment of me. "Took your advice and got rid of those nags I had been stabling on the post roads. My bank account is the better for it. If Philmot don't get your diamonds back, I want to make reparation for it. You have saved this family a deal of grief by giving us an excuse to turn Harmsworth off."

"I would have done better to tell you about him before leaving, but could not like to disparage him till I was sure it was not all a misunderstanding. I had no idea Alice meant to have him."

"Very proper of you. But then it comes as no surprise that Miss Fenwick behaves with propriety."

It was as close to an apology as he meant to come, and closer than I either expected or deserved. "I was a great burden to you, Lord Synge," I admitted with a rueful smile.

"Oh as to that, it is Philmot that has been a burden ever since you left. He has jawed our ears off to write and ask you back. I wonder why that would be, eh Miss Fenwick?" he asked with a meaningful wink.

"I expect he is having trouble to find another secretary and wants to hire me again. You can tell him for me I am not interested. He made me work too hard. You and your wife were better employers."

He chose to take this as a famous joke. When we went into dinner he offered me his arm, though he ought by rights to have taken Doris. She went with Papa and Lady Synge. Alice was not at the table. After dinner,

Lady Synge suggested I go up to see her and Dottie.

"I am ashamed to let Alice be seen in public, with her eyes as red as a ferret's. You must talk some sense into her, Miss Fenwick. She always minded you."

I heartily wished she had not minded me so well, especially my advice to accept Harmsworth. I knew I would not be welcome with Alice. Dottie, dear thing, broke right into sobs and threw herself on my breast. I confess a tear gathered in my own eye, to see her so moved, and so happy to see me. Alice was less ecstatic. She wore a sullen pout, with her eyes the shade described by her mama.

"I thought you would be smiling, to know you do not have to marry Harmsworth," I said to cheer her.

It precipitated a fresh bout of sniffles, through which a disjointed story slowly emerged. Clearly her life was blighted if Captain Tierney could not learn she was not to marry her lord.

"He will learn it. It will be published no later than tomorrow. Your father has sent the notices to the papers."

"Robbie still won't ask me to marry him," she said, her gulps diminishing.

"Why do you say so?"

"Oh Miss Fenwick, it is all *your* fault. If you had not told me I was too good for him, I would not have acted so horrid. He says I am *spoiled,* and not fit to—to be an officer's wife, for I have not enough backbone. And now he is going to be a *major!*" she added, looking to see how the demanding governess was impressed with this promotion in his status.

I allowed myself to be greatly impressed, and soon to see a resemblance between his progress and that of the Duke of Wellington. She would clearly be a duchess within a twelvemonth. "If he reads the papers and finds out I am not to marry Harmsworth," she added, with a fresh trickle out of the corner of her eyes.

"Well now it seems to me an officer's wife ought not to cry like a baby. Someone is bound to tell him." I said no more till I discovered whether the parents were still opposed to the match.

I had the pleasure of seeing her sniffles stop, and her shoulders straighten up before turning to my more agreeable charge, Dottie, to hear how she was keeping up her reading program without me. I stayed with them an hour, having to tear myself away to rejoin the adults below. When I stepped on to the landing, Philmot was just being shown in. I felt a strong urge to turn on my heels and run back upstairs, but as he had fixed a challenging gray eye on me, I was forced to continue my descent.

Chapter Twenty-one

PHILMOT LOOKED NO HAPPIER at the encounter than myself. He wore a scowl, which cheered me insensibly. "Good evening, Philmot. In your customary high spirits, I see. You must have deserted your dinner party rather abruptly."

"It's about time you showed up!" was his first remark, uttered in an angry voice.

"Had I realized Alice was favoring Harmsworth's suit I would have been here sooner."

"I'm not talking about that!"

"Are you not? I should like to have a word with you about it all the same, before we join the others. I feel so culpable in the affair I wish to help Alice patch it up with her officer. Can you tell me something about him?"

"Is it possible you shared a roof with her for so long without learning about him?"

"I did not encourage her to speak about him to me. It was poorly done on my part. No need to tell me so. What sort of a fellow is he?"

"A younger son of a younger son with no prospects but what he makes for himself in the army."

"The army can provide a good career. He is to be made a major already."

"He's bright and a worker. Hardly a connection to delight her parents."

"I am sorry to hear it. I hoped for a happy ending. Is it out of the question entirely?"

"Alice has a reasonable dowry. The boy is of good family and character. The mood Synge is in, I think the latter is of considerable importance to him. Between us—Synge and myself I mean—we might advance his career."

My hopes rose at this encouraging speech. "I hope he reads of the broken engagement in tomorrow's papers then."

"I am surprised the thorough Miss Fenwick would leave it to chance. I sent a note over to headquarters several hours ago. If he is not here yet, I assume he is on night duty, and will be over at the crack of dawn, battering down the door. I expect between the pair of them they'll wear down any resistance that still remains. Of more interest to me at the moment is this business of Harmsworth trotting off with your diamonds. Why did you not tell me?"

"It had nothing to do with you," I said in a dismissing way, turning towards the saloon. I was detained by a hard grasp on the wrist.

"You were living under my roof at the time, and under my protection. I feel responsible."

"I was with Synge when it happened."

"You mentioned Squibbs's place, if I am not mistaken."

"Yes."

"What was the date exactly?"

"The date is on the chit. It was shortly after I bought Lady Beaton's carriage."

The introduction of this name into our conversation had the effect of putting us both on our high ropes. We walked towards the saloon. We were soon parted to sit in two separate groups: the men on one side discussing the important and interesting matters, while the ladies listened politely and occasionally ventured a word. There was no hoping for any rapport between Doris and Lady Synge. They might have been of two different species for all they had in common. I feared Papa must be similarly out of place with the men, and was surprised to see he was very much a part of that group. The younger gentlemen were consulting him, listening to his words with apparent interest. I noted in particular that Philmot treated him with not only respect, but deference.

It was not till the tea tray arrived that the two sexes got together. By then, our immediate fates had been decided. The Fenwick family was to spend a short time at Philmot's home, while our host and Papa busied themselves to recover the necklace. I had a strong wish to dissuade Papa from accepting Philmot's hospitality.

Philmot knew it too. He looked at me several times while it was outlined.

"I expect Doris would prefer to be downtown at the hotel, Papa, for shopping and so on," I mentioned.

"My carriage will be at your disposal, Ma'am," Philmot said to Doris.

This attention threw her into a tizzy. She blushed like a schoolgirl, while thanking him three or four times. Undismayed, he took up a position at her elbow. Anyone of the least sensitivity could see she was discomfited by his presence, his insistence on conversing with her. I could not understand why he had selected this least conversable member of the party for his particular companion. For a good quarter of an hour they talked together, with Doris's tongue finally loosening up to reveal God knows what intimate details of our life at Bath. The one speech I managed to overhear during a lull in Lady Synge's inconsequential gossip was that "Livvie persuaded me to leave off the feathers." No doubt he was keenly interested to hear this piece of information.

When we took our leave, it had been decided we would spend the night at the hotel, going to Philmot's place in the morning. "They seem like good people," was Papa's opinion as we drove through the night. "Synge is not a deep man, nor a great reader, but young Philmot is certainly a man of parts."

Papa could have no notion one of those parts was pure lecher. What would he think if he ever discovered it? "He is very nice," Doris seconded the opinion. "Easy to chat to. Not what I expected at all from the proud look of him. He recommended we try Lattimers for bonnets, Olivia."

I tried for a few more details of their conversation, but concluded the sole topic had been sartorial.

212

Nine thirty was an early hour to be landing in on our host the next morning, but when we had been up for two full hours, I could delay Papa no longer. "Philmot said we would get an early start," he insisted. "He will have been waiting an hour. Drink up your coffee, do, Livvie." I drank up my coffee.

Philmot was still sipping his when we arrived. He left a full cup on the table. Doris and I were turned over to the servants while the gentlemen went after Harmsworth. It was amusing to watch Doris's head turn from side to side as we were led up to our rooms. I was just putting aside my bonnet when she knocked and came in. "There's a servant in my room insisting she will unpack my bag!" she whispered in horrified accents.

"Let her. It is the custom in the homes of the mighty."

"What will she think of my flannelette nightgown?"

"She will wish she had one half so fine I expect."

"Oh, and your papa's small clothes all mended!" she replied.

"A shocking thing, for a servant to see mended clothing!"

"Easy for *you*. You are accustomed to this sort of thing. I am very uncomfortable here, but at least it is not costing your papa anything."

"You must own the rooms are finer than at the hotel, Doris," I pointed out. Mine was also a good deal finer than the one given me when an employee, I noticed. My remark only served to make Doris put her fingers to her lips in her old annoying way. "Let us go downstairs and say how do you do to Philmot's aunt."

This proved to be the best idea I had throughout the entire trip. The two were cut from the same bolt. Miss Millichope was delighted to have a provincial to condescend to, and Doris able to cope with the condescension of a mind so similar to her own. She flushed with pleasure at Miss Millichope's approval of her house-keeping chores, nodding with interest to hear she could save fifty percent by buying in bulk. Just what bulk could produce this enormous saving for a household of three people was not explained. We chatted the morning away, lunched together, and were taken to Bond Street for an orgy of buying sewing pins and needles in bulk in the afternoon. After saving fifty percent of a half crown by this wise shopping, Doris was permitted to go to Lattimers to look at bonnets, which Miss Millichope told her were too expensive for a Dean's wife. "You would not want to give a bad example of peacockery to your parishioners," she was told.

"Indeed no," Doris agreed sadly.

While they came to this holy conclusion, I quietly ordered the bonnet to be delivered to me, and paid for it. Doris took a girlish and sinful pleasure in the stunt when I sneaked it into her room later.

"We will be dining at home this evening," Miss Millichope informed us later. "Philmot has cancelled his engagements for the remainder of the week to be at your disposal. It was very kind of him," she told Doris, who hardly knew what to say to such an announcement.

Her perfectly sincere "I wish he had not!" was accepted as polite gratitude.

Not only the Synges but Major Tierney as well came to Hanover Square to dine that evening. Alice was effulgent; there is no other word to describe the glow that shone in her eyes. The major was hardly less so. "We are to be married!" were the first words she spoke to me. "Only Mama says we must allow a decent time to elapse before it is announced, because of my other engagement. Isn't it *wonderful,* Miss Fenwick?"

"I couldn't be happier for you both!" I agreed, giving her a hug.

"You will love—like Robbie better when you come to know him, his many excellent qualities, even if he is not a lord," she added.

Out of the mouth of this near-babe I heard how disgusting my old philosophy sounded. Her fiancé was still a trifle stiff with me, which did not detract an iota from my improved opinion of him.

Dottie was allowed to attend this small party, to celebrate her return to health. "Next year you may be congratulating me, and wishing me well, Miss Fenwick. I am to make my bows next season, since Alice has been bounced off this year."

"Be sure to write and let me know all about your young man when the time comes," I told her.

"We shall keep in touch regularly," she promised.

My diamonds were not forgotten in the visit. "I have been to see Squibbs. He says your necklace was purchased by a Mr. Enders, from Brighton," Philmot explained when we had a chance for a little private talk in a corner.

"Did he say what price Harmsworth got for them?"

"A hundred guineas, on a straight sale. He never tried to pawn them at all."

"How did he think he could get away with it?" I asked, astonished at his recklessness. I had already come to terms with his lack of character.

"He very nearly did, didn't he? I suppose he counted on your discretion to keep it secret, or perhaps he felt it was a question of your word against his, as you did not exact any written receipt from him when you handed the diamonds over. Rather remiss of you, incidentally."

"Who would ever have thought a lord would sink so low?"

"Certainly not you. I shall go to Brighton tomorrow and try if I can find Enders."

"Papa will get the money. I appreciate all your efforts on my behalf, Philmot. We don't want you spending your blunt besides."

"I shall submit a detailed bill when I return. It is not likely Enders will turn them over for the price he paid. He will expect a profit on the business," Philmot cautioned, unable to hide his relish. What sum would be asked, I wondered, and would Papa be able to raise it?

"If he wants too much . . ." I said hesitantly.

"An expensive business, trusting your fortune to a nobleman," he remarked idly.

The next morning Papa and Philmot set off for Brighton early. Lady Synge took us for a drive in the park in the morning, then returned after luncheon with a few ladies to pay a call. "You remember Miss Fenwick, who was visiting me earlier in the season," she reminded Lady Hazelton.

"The lady who was governess to your Dottie, is it not?" the dame asked, raising a lorgnette to examine me.

"Governess?" Lady Synge laughed archly. "Say friend rather. Olivia was kind enough to lend me a hand in the schoolroom when my Miss Silver had to leave unexpectedly."

I had difficulty to keep my face composed when I heard my christian name fall from her lips, along with that whisker about my being a guest. "Olivia is interested in progressive education," she rattled on. "Her cousin, Lady Monterne, put the bug in her ear when she was staying at Dawlish last year. How is the dear Marchioness, Olivia?"

The talk continued, bringing in the Strathaconas and the Duchess of Tavistock. They paid more than a formal visit. For over an hour we all sat in the saloon, sipping sherry, eating biscuits, and pretending we were not all ill at ease throughout the charade. Miss Millichope and Doris were also present, but as they said little, I have not mentioned them. Doris was being introduced into the realm of chapbooks, and other murky intellectual waters by her new mentor.

Chapter Twenty-two

I RECEIVED MY DIAMONDS back that evening from Papa. "Rough going we had of it with that Enders fellow," he told me, with a reprimanding shake of the head. "He is a dealer in gems, secondhand pieces of jewelry he picks up where he can, without too much concern for where they came from, or by what means. He wanted plenty for them, I can tell you."

"How much?" I asked, dreading to hear the answer.

"A hundred and fifty, but Philmot took high ground, threatening to bring in the law and speaking of 'stolen jewelry' and so on. In the end, the man was happy enough to part with them at the price he paid. It was our having a lord to represent us that saved the day. Simple folks hold them in awe, as Philmot said." My eyes narrowed at this. "Had it been just you and me, Livvie, we would have paid more."

"*You* paid him, I hope? You did not let Philmot pay?"

"I hadn't the cash on me. I am to make arrangements to pay him after I get home to my bank."

This distressing news was digested. "We can go home tomorrow," I said. "The money can be sent back next day. I shall pay you back by installment from my own money. In fact, I can sell my tilbury."

"Philmot says you cannot continue driving it." He cast a wise, sorry look at me.

"He told you why?"

"I heard the whole. Shocking way to carry on. He says those days are over for him, however."

If this were true, it was superfluous of Philmot to have bothered raising the point at all. I could not but wonder whether the matter of character had arisen with regard to another offer to myself. Papa did not say so, nor did I have the courage to inquire.

There was no company to dinner that evening, just the household and the Fenwicks. After dinner the scene in the small parlor to which we adjourned held very much the air of a family gathering. The gentlemen perused the newspapers, the ladies sat across from them talking, sipping tea, and peeping from time to time to see if the men's cups wanted filling.

"I see Reverend Crombie is speaking this week," Philmot pointed out to my father. "Two evenings from now, at the Theological Society. You ought to stay and hear him, Mr. Fenwick. He has some interesting views on . . ." he took another look at his newspaper, "on the matter of double and treble livings. A bad business, that."

"So it is. I think you want to appoint a new minister for that living you spoke of. I could recommend half a dozen to you. Crombie, eh? I would like to see him. I have known him any time these thirty years."

"We ought to be getting home," I reminded him.

"So we should. Two evenings from now, you say, Philmot?"

"Yes, only two. It would be a pity to miss him. I think you should stay."

"I would certainly like to see him."

"You cannot be thinking of leaving already!" Miss Millichope declared, incensed. "You said a week at least, Philmot. I have cancelled everything for a week. Doris and I have a drive planned for tomorrow afternoon. She wants to see Carlton House and the cathedral. She has never seen Carlton House, imagine! It would be a shame to come to London and not see the cathedral."

"You want to see the Tower of London and Whitehall while you are here," Philmot added, turning to converse with the elder ladies. "There are any number of famous sights to see. The mint . . ."

"We couldn't begin to do it in one day," Mrs. Millichope pointed out.

"No, no. A week at least."

No amount of private persuading could prevent Papa and Doris from their course. The ladies were off to see the sights, and Papa to see Dr. Crombie, who had soon drawn him into a group of visiting churchmen who had many activities to be shared. I was left alone to indulge my frustration to the top of my bent. We were falling deeper and deeper into Philmot's debt with the passing of each day. Of all the people in London, he was the last I would wish to be indebted to. I went out a few times with the Synges, *mère* and *filles*. I sat alone over coffee one morning after Doris and Miss Millichope and Papa had left. Philmot was nowhere about. I wondered whether he was still in bed, or had left.

"His lordship would like to see you in his study when you are finished, Ma'am," the servant told me.

What a wave of memories washed over me as I knocked at that tall oaken door. I wondered if he had got a new secretary. If not, I might be of some help to him in the interim, to reduce our debt of gratitude to him. The door into Harding's and my old office stood ajar, showing me an empty chair at the desk.

"Come in, Olivia," he said.

I entered, expecting to be offered a chair. Instead he strolled to the back windows, with the uninteresting view. I walked along with him. "I know you are upset over this business of repaying me for the diamonds, and have a solution to suggest. How would you like to sell me back Lady Beaton's tilbury?"

"I would be happy to be rid of it. Has she smashed up her high perch phaeton, or do you have another lady in mind to receive it?"

"Another young lady," he replied nonchalantly, but he could not quite keep a smile from peeping out.

"Congratulations. That didn't take long."

"Oh she's not my mistress. Did your father not tell you I am all reformed? It's for Alice. She will want to be setting up a little carriage now she is to be a married lady. I'll have it painted to disguise its lurid past and give it to her as a wedding gift. I can return your hundred guineas."

"No, no. You must keep them to pay for the necklace."

"Well yes—that was my meaning. I'll be happy to take the nags off your hands as well, if you like."

"Excellent. I'll have them sent from Bath. I am sorry we are imposing so long on your hospitality."

"No apology is necessary. I know you have changed some of your thinking lately, but I hope you have not lost the use of your wits for all that. You know it was my doing that you come here, and stay for a while. You cannot be in the dark as to my reason for doing so."

"I realize you are trying to re-establish me to respectability. I am thankful, but it is not at all necessary."

"I don't want to marry a scarlet lady," he said, reaching for my hands. I walked quickly away from the window towards the desk.

"You have made this offer before, Philmot. You know I . . ."

"Not this one," he said, coming quickly towards me. I retreated behind his desk, with his lordship in hot pursuit. "I made a damned presumptuous ass of myself in Hans Town. You quite rightly swatted me down. This time I have a different proposal to make." I continued retreating, till I hit the corner. "Don't bother looking over your shoulder. There is no escape," he said, "unless you mean to crawl into the cabinet and bolt the door behind you."

"I'll take *these* in custody, for my own defence," he said, closing his fingers tightly over mine. "I never was slapped by a woman before. It infuriated me to such an extent . . ."

"You deserved it."

"Yes, a just dessert I agree. But isn't it time for the savory yet, Olivia?" he asked, drawing my hands around his waist. Before I had time to remove them, I was crushed in a merciless embrace. I had to open my eyes once to confirm it was really the aloof Philmot performing with such boyish enthusiasm, then I could participate more fully. After a long and passionate kiss he lifted his head and smiled.

"*Very* competent," he congratulated me. "I would have to give that an A grade. As I should have expected."

"Of the clever Miss Fenwick," I added.

221

Let COVENTRY Give You
A Little Old-Fashioned Romance

GREAT ADVENTURES IN READING

THE MONA INTERCEPT   14374 $2.75
by Donald Hamilton
A story of the fight for power, life, and love on the treacherous seas.

JEMMA   14375 $2.75
by Beverly Byrne
*A glittering Cinderella story set against the background of Lincoln's
America, Victoria's England, and Napolean's France.*

DEATH FIRES   14376 $1.95
by Ron Faust
*The questions of art and life become a matter of life and death on
a desolate stretch of the Mexican coast.*

PAWN OF THE OMPHALOS   14377 $1.95
by E. C. Tubb
*A lone man agrees to gamble his life to obtain the scientific data
that might save a planet from destruction.*

DADDY'S LITTLE HELPERS   14384 $1.50
by Bil Keane
More laughs with The Family Circus crew.

Buy them at your local bookstore or use this handy coupon for ordering.

This offer expires 1 September 81   8106

NEW FROM FAWCETT CREST